Without a Name

Without a Name

a novel

Yvonne Vera

TSAR
Toronto
1995

The publishers acknowledge generous assistance
from the Canada Council and the Ontario Arts Council.

First published in 1994 by Baobab Books, Harare, Zimbabwe.

Canadian Cataloguing in Publication Data

Vera, Yvonne
    Without a name

ISBN 0-920661-54-8

I. Title.

PS8593.E73W58 1995   C813'.54   C95-932507-7
PR9199.3.V47W58   1995

Printed and bound in Canada

TSAR Publications
P. O. Box 6996, Station A
Toronto, Ontario M5W 1X7
Canada

For my mother
and her mother

1

Heat mauled the upturned faces.

The bus was fierce red. Skin turned a violent mauve. That is how hot the day was. The faces jostled and hurried, surrounding the bus with shimmering voices. The large black wheels were yellow with gathered dust. Mud had dried in the wide grooves within the tires. Small stones looked out from the mud. Thick layers of brown earth covered the windows and the rest of the body, but the bus still shone red. It was that red. It was so stunningly red it was living.

Mazvita separated herself from the waiting red of the bus, colour so sharp it cut into her thought like lightning. Merciless, that red. It was an everywhere red which cracked the white and black shell of her eyes. Heat thundered beneath her feet. She retreated. She stood apart, anxious, waiting for the doors of the bus to burst open. She watched the door closed tightly against her entry. The bus sat in a rippling lake of rising heat and dust. The dust sucked the water from her eyes.

"Nothing to load onto the bus?" the voice swooped towards her. It did not wait for an answer but swept past and landed on the trembling roof of the bus; it belonged to an agile black shape fastening beds, caged chickens, maize sacks, chairs and tables. The pile on the bus was growing steadily.

The bus shook, and sagged. The bus sat still. A loud shout rang through the air, concerning a mattress about to fall. The shape that was the conductor, left one end of the bus and slid to the back, pulled hard at something grey hanging and heavy, retrieved it, and tied it straight down the roof.

Mazvita saw the faces hurry, heard a murmuring like boiling water. The voices swirled like a flood to one end of the bus where there was space left to haul one more article. A bed was raised high towards the roof, brought forward, tied down. It was lost among the many pieces already struggling there. Jarring, voices scrambled and jostled. Cries converged, called, and retreated.

Mazvita felt the intense heat which circled her with the simmering voices and brought the red glow of the bus to her face. The ominous hue spread down her arms, and sought her fingers. She stood still. She stood near the bus shelter, but not beneath it, a metal roof held up by four high wooden poles. She stood still. She stood next to one of the poles, on the outside. She stood on the outside. She stood alone.

Beneath the dim shed, children had been left to guard the smaller possessions which would be carried onto the bus but their attention wandered as soon as the bus enveloped their mothers in its vibrant shade. They exploded. They ran around the shelter, screeched and scattered. They laughed, because one of them had fallen down. The shed was full of their delight. They rescued each other from beneath fallen bags which, filled to capacity, tore open on their collapse. A red scarf lay trampled on the ground. It wove itself around a bare tiny foot, and the figure fell again in a knotted cry, but the children had discovered the secret of their freedom; there was no need for caution or restraint. There were no pauses to their joy which resounded in one continuous voice, a tender elegant quiver pure and plain. The children found gaps between the rays of the sun and ran through them, their tiny bodies supple, carried on pattering flirtatious feet, in faltering voices that embraced their yearning for enchanting discoveries. They found narrow and untrodden paths. The children had a limitless tenacity for dream, a flowing capacity to wander wide and far. They were children.

They emerged from their escape in a myriad of joy, their faces covered with their gaiety, bright with their phenomenal journeying. They held out their cupped hands above their heads and gathered the joy that tumbled from the sun, which swooped down their throats. Blue lizard tails disappeared beneath the grey roof of the shed, vanished between their fingers which were spread out to the sky. They ran back quickly into the shed, gurgling, their fingers still surprised, burning and tingling. They filled their dreams with unformed desires, with tentative aspirations, with timid bliss. They bathed in an exhilarating caress of innocent and weariless joy. Then they fell on the split bags, and slept an accented sleep.

The shrieks reached Mazvita, climbed over her shoulders to her back, receded. She felt a violent throbbing cross her forehead, and lifted a limp hand to wipe the water from her face. Drops fell from behind her ears, slid slowly down, trickled beyond her shoulders to her back. The water traced a convoluted path over her tired skin. She passed the back of her right hand across her neck and spread the warm sweat over her arm, over the loose skin. Her neck was twisted. A bone at the bottom of her neck told her that her neck had been turned and turned till it could no longer find a resting place. Her neck had been broken. She felt a violent piercing like shattered glass, on her tongue where she carried fragments of her being.

There was a lump growing on the side of her neck. A sagging grew with the lump, so that her body leaned to the left, following the heavy lump. She could no longer swallow even her saliva which settled in one huge lump in her throat. Whatever she swallowed moved to one side of her body. She had lost her centre, the centre in which her thoughts had found anchor. She was amazed at how quickly the past vanished.

The lump had swallowed her thoughts, she decided. She blamed this lump for her inability to think clear thoughts. It swelled endlessly, this lump, and she leaned her head further towards her lowered shoulder, as though she needed a new angle to her reality, an untried advantage, her eyes quiet, tucked upward beneath her eyelids. She peered at her reality. Some unusual sight had appeared before her, gripped her face and smeared it with mud. The mud had dried in angry and repeated streaks across her whole face, over her lips, her forehead and held her in a puzzled and frenzied stare.

She nursed an elbow gently in her palm, and waited anxiously. The lump lay between her ear and her shoulder. She felt it growing there in repeated outward pushes. She had no doubt that all her body was moving slowly into that lump, that she would eventually turn to find her whole being had abandoned her, rushed into that space beside her neck, for she heard voices there. She heard a faint dying cry. The fingers on her left hand curved slowly upward.

Her skin peeled off, parting from her body. She had suffered so much that her skin threatened to fall pitilessly to the ground. It hung from below her neck, from her arms, from her whole silent body. The skin pulled away from her in the intense dry heat. She felt it pull from her shoulders. She screamed, her arms and elbows bare. The sky tore with her scream, for a dark cloud appeared suddenly over her eyes, blinding her. The skin fell from her back. She was left stripped, exposed, bare wide across her back.

She leaned backwards, her eyes astonished.

∞∞

2

They had spoken, among the mushrooms.

The mushrooms stood meek beneath the decaying log that was partly buried in the ground, and she had bent forward and touched them fearfully, touched their floating beauty for they seemed ready to break, seemed waiting to break if they were touched. They were white beneath the cold black shadow, the wet earth, the decay. They were a radiant white like drops of daylight. Their rim touched the ground with a curving soft shell. A dark soil grew threateningly over the feathery shelter of the mushroom.

Mazvita had moved from the brightness to the shadow and the shadow was so sudden and heavy like water thrown over her arms, over her whole waiting body that she shivered at the water that fell from the tree not in drops, but in a sudden spilling, like the mushrooms which she sighted when she turned her face laughing and gay, seeking to find him. The water pulled at her arms in thick and heavy waves. It felt heavy over her arms. She moved eagerly towards the log.

A lush greenness spread to the ground. It was wet there, and the ground was soft. The large tree glistened with wide thickly veined leaves. The leaves were rounded partings of green moon. The trunk stood firm and straight, with a smooth grey surface. The bark was wound in stiff tightening circles spiralling to the base, disappearing in a mound of weaving roots that swirled angrily from the ground. Within the roots, which formed small channels and basins, was held some water with a swarm of brown decaying leaves. Branches grew outward, flattened, spread and created a broad dark circle, a wide shelter. Her shoulders tingled with the suddenness of the cold. She looked up at the merging leaves where there was no sky; the shadow cleansed her. There was no sky under the tree.

The laughing made her curious and careless, made her want to pull at the mushrooms, so she reached her thumb and forefinger ever so delicately, and held the soft cushiony head, held it so gently, feeling already the grooved underneath so tender and the surface above so smooth that her finger slid over the head past the grooves and met a thin polished stem, soft, then she held that stem tight but gentle, pulled at it tight, but gentle. The ground was soft and yielding.

There was nothing like pulling that mushroom. It accepted her gentle hand, followed her in a long slow quiver and the stem grew out of the ground into her palm. White. The neck was smooth and waiting and soft. She felt the softness linger between her fingers, slippery, fragile. The soil crept beneath her nails.

It was after she held it in her palm that she saw the brown spots within the grooves, the spots that spread to the smooth surface of the mushroom, a sad brown quite unexpected. The tinge spread downward, towards the neck. She felt the loss of that whiteness and longed for the bright sun, away from the cold shade. Above her she heard the leaves move softly over each other. She held the neck of the mushroom between her fingers. She looked up and searched beneath the cold leaves for a waiting sky.

Nyenyedzi caught up with her. She saw him come and held out the mushroom to him, and he took it and crushed it, crushed its soft head.

"It could be poisonous," Nyenyedzi said. He crushed the mushroom against her palm, with his right hand. "I will find mushrooms for you, if you want some. This mushroom is not for eating."

I wasn't going to eat it," she shrugged her shoulders. "I only wanted to touch it. It felt so good to hold it. Why did you crush it?"

"There are many under the log." He kicked at the log. It surrendered decay, turned hollow. Crumbled pieces fell towards the soft heads of the mushrooms below, tarnishing them. She wanted to gather the mushrooms towards her. She held out her palm, but did not move. She remembered the mushroom he had crushed. She held out a trembling palm. She was hopeful.

He named her. He reminded her of what they had found together, for he had held her, and she had grown towards him, yielded from the ground into his palm.

It was not difficult.

The blaze she felt amazed her when all there was afterward was a lingering wet and delicate softness beneath her. She smelt the decaying leaves surrounding the rotting log, and kept the crushed mushroom in her hand as he found her waiting, found her. The stem was still whole, a neck closed and rounded. She was grateful he had not broken the neck and held it tight within her fingers. Her palm grew warm.

He touched her below her neck, above her firm breasts, and she curled her arm over his back, rested her hand there. She rested a closed hand over his back where a thin trickling sweat met her fingers. With her other hand she gathered the warmth beneath his arm and spread it in slow deliberate motions across his back. She listened. She heard the leaves turn silent. She listened. She heard him murmur "*Howa*". She was sure he had called.

"Is that what you called me?" Mazvita asked, thrilled, surprised, still longing.

"I don't remember. Is that what I called you?"

"You said *Howa*, twice. I'm sure I heard you. Is that what you called me?"

"I called you... *Howa*." He laughed.

In the future Nyenyedzi evoked that name when he wanted to hold her close, like today. She always thought of the spotless white mushrooms she had not found.

He held her. He brought to her soft dying mushrooms, the ones she had found.

∞∞

3

The white aprons hung on a corner of the street. Two wooden pegs had selected one wide square apron and pinned it along a small wire held between two poles, one of them a parking metre which said in a red flash 'expired'. There was a bright red car parked there. The other pole was a small boy's arm. He stood as though in possession of a secret. He was quite still for such a strenuous and monotonous task. He stood as though frightened to move. The woman seller cast unkind glances at him. He held one end of the white apron, so that it opened very wide, and the wind blew on one side of it, and it curved inward as though in anticipation of the baby.

The back of the apron was heavily stitched turning it into a firmly padded support. The back was starched, cracked like bark. Somewhere the white thread had run out and the tailor had employed a black thread. This black thread ran frantically through the borders of the white apron, zig-zagging. It was meant to be endearing, but the suddenness of the contrasting thread held the eyes in a furrowed gaze. It was truly surprising.

The boy had tied the bottom of this ingenious apron to this right leg. The boy simply stood, as though it was in his nature to stand. His feet were planted firmly on the ground. His hair stood in proud and independent strands all over his head. One arm hung limply above the pocket of his torn shorts. One could have walked forward, and put a coin through his ear. He was the same height as the metre, equally still. The metre was silver grey, so was the boy. Perhaps he had not eaten for days, months, maybe years – he competed with the metre for thinness. The apron shone a dramatic white against the boy's thinness, against his face dull and grey.

People pushed and shoved as though they had no eyes to see. It was 1977, what else was there to do but push forward. Mazvita walked quickly through the impassive faces, in a tunnel of her own where it was truly unlit, desperately narrow. She sent her head forward through the tunnel and met a darkness tall and consuming, where she could not turn or speak or see. She could no longer move her head forward because the pain threatened to collapse her whole body, to sink her into the ground, to bury her. She held her head in a definite yet unaccountable stare.

In an instant, she had turned blind, the blindness rose from inside her and overwhelmed her entire face. She no longer spoke. Mute and wounded she moved through the streets and wept. Her weeping fell in silent drops into her cupped palms. The streets grew rich with showers, with her tears.

Mazvita turned from one end of the street into another, and the aprons greeted her. "Apron *Amai*! Apron *Amai*!" A commodious and enterprising woman shouted at her as she turned, as though she expected her. It was the first voice Mazvita recognized since morning. The voice was anxious and pressing.

Mazvita bought the apron in a state of quiet nervousness. Her fingers trembled, not yet certain whether to confess or escape. Some kinds of truths long for the indifferent face of a stranger, such truths love that face from the neck up, from the forehead down. There is little to remember in a face with which no intimacy has been shared, to which there is no kinship. There is nothing to lose between strangers, absolutely no risk of being contaminated by another's emotion; there are no histories shared, no promises made, no hopes conjured and affirmed. Only faces offered, in improbable disguises, promising freedom.

The apron was made of strong cotton material. In this matter, Mazvita was not going to take any chances. She had regretfully unfolded four lonely silver coins from a dirty handkerchief held in a crumpled lump between her fingers. She had purchased the apron in the middle of a busy indifferent street.

Her fingers, as they handed the coins over, loved the stranger's face. They caressed that strangeness anonymously, confided in that absent sensibility. Mazvita's fingers folded and unfolded while waiting for the apron to be unhooked from the fence. The seller imagined that this particular apron was what this particular stranger wanted, because she had moved determinedly towards that apron. But Mazvita had only moved forward because she felt like falling down, felt like spreading her arms wide. Mazvita searched the woman's face as she prepared the apron. Mazvita stood still.

The boy kept his arm up. Morsels of freedom desperately snatched were bitter, soaked with a remorseful after-taste. It was not worth the effort, the risk.

Mazvita moved on, the apron folded close to her breast. She looked for an unlit passage.

∞∞

4

An egg, the brown of its tone, the unforgettable pale invitation of its colour, the maze of its smells, the promise of fragility like anxious tenderness. The rainbow of its smoothendearing surface, elegant, its echoes slender and oval. Its promises hidden but complete, its palm-nestling size, a shy silent awakening. Supple and wholesome.

He held her hand and walked between the rocks where the earth was dry, leaving the egg where they had found it. The bird had built a nest in a crevice within the rock.

"Mazvita," he said freely.

The rocks towered above them, near and rounded. Underneath were dull shelters. Dense shadows cast by the looming stones, like smoke. The rocks were smooth. Brittle and jagged stones peeled off the rocks and fell to the ground. Mazvita and Nyenyedzi walked out to a rock that was spread on the ground. Short green leaves grew between meandering cracks. Within the hard stone were the tight swollen roots of trees, and desperate waving stems of slowly growing plants.

Mazvita pulled Nyenyedzi down beneath the rocks which had been warmed by the sun, and felt the warmth rise over her naked back. She held him in a succumbing gasp, then folded his head over her chest. She felt the hardened skin of his knee over her pelvis, felt it scratch briefly beneath her navel. The knee pressed down on her, but not painfully. So she passed a tender finger through his hair. He lay between her fingers. She closed her eyes against the blue that fell from the sky into her eyes and she heard a sentinel on a rock cry loud, a piercing cry that beat against her ears.

The sentinel cried yet again, slow and chasing, one call calling another. The sky overwhelmed her with a lithe blue hanging over her eyebrows, so near her breath embraced it. The blue pulled her up into the sky, and she called softly to tell him about a translucent shiver that tumbled from the sky, about the daze that lulled her in a horizon prolific with caressing yellow rays, about the warmth rippling over her knees, but he smoothed her stomach in tender fond waves and she forgot about the blue of the sky about his knee about ... She was breathless with an ancient longing. He smoothed her back with a kind tongue, blue and large like the sky. She felt a brilliant cascading joy. A calm modest thrill sent an even pressure to her palm then circled her bent wrists, resting in the wet spaces between her fingers. She felt the ground, exquisite, pressed at the back of her feet. The blue brimmed and soared around her. She was restored in a pleated sky.

He moved above her in lilting repeated spasms. He held her very close, wiped her forehead in gentle beseeching strokes. He rested a solid arm on the ground above the soft curve of her shoulder, beside her ear. She felt the inside of his arm rub firmly against her, along her neck. He was content with her presence. Their eyes met in a silence rich with imaginings, with a brave ecstasy. He was heavy where he rested above her, but even in that she found an exultation so complete and final, an ease unquestionable, a profuse tenderness. There was no beginning or ending to her happiness, only a continuous whirl of blue cloud. The air was bright and clear beneath the sky, transparent. A dazzling shower of bright stars fell from the sky.

She was comforted. They lay still in a triumphant arch, under the spread hem of the horizon, intertwined. They lay in a whispering veil of white and lucid cloud.

She remembered the egg, whole, nestling on her palm.

∞∞

5

Harari.

Mazvita found a welcoming alley between two towering brick buildings. The alley was narrow and cramped. *Nyore Nyore* – one side of the walls promised falsely. A thick smoke descended into the constricting crevice, and swallowed some of the letters. The bricks had turned from bright red to a rapid black brown. *Nyore Nyore.* Letters shouted, struggled beneath growing layers of plastering smoke. It was that kind of era. An easy wealth was promised, an easy love, an easy life, an easy death. *Nyore Nyore.* The alley smelt of tentative promises quickly betrayed. It smelt of urine.

A frayed leather purse lay abandoned on the edge of the building. A black hat, the brim torn off, curled stiffly upward. Pigeons fluttered grey spotted wings and flew from the entrapping cavern, frightened by her feet. They returned, retreating behind the set of lined metal garbage cans. Wings settled into a slow cloying palpitation.

Mazvita met empty cans of tinned beans where broken bottles littered the narrow path, amid the garbage cans. One can folded in the middle. It had been thrust into the alley in one heaving and merciless manoeuvre. The wall had met it with equal indifference. The world vacillated with clamour. Recognition was easy, calm, tumultuous. Poverty was not a secret, otherwise what was there to clamber out of? It was necessary to be poor. It made people long for a long day full of greetings.

The pigeons beat a sorrowful liturgy with rippling wings and quivering feet. They sent brittle cries that soaked into the mounds of metal rubble. Mazvita walked gingerly through the mounting debris, casting one brief glance over her shoulder. She heard a cat leap in the dark onto the roof of the *Nyore Nyore* building. Wood lay discarded in the alley, some broken furniture, a broken chair with one leg missing, and the seat fatally collapsed. The chair had been mangled. One half of its back-rest had folded forward, unable to sustain the havoc on its frame.

Mazvita stood amid the wreckage, halfway through the dimness. She searched the brittle ground. She witnessed people walk past each end of the alley. The people lasted only two quick steps before they disappeared on either side. Her reality was that brief and intermittent. She gasped at her vision full of chaos. The people dwindled into mere shades of colour and cloud. She thought she saw an umbrella walk by. Just like that. Then she saw a soldier. It frightened her to see the soldier. He must have a gun. After all it was 1977. Guns were pointed to the sky.

She hated the city and its commitment to a wild and stultifying indifference. She pulled her eyes from the streets, from the stilted portions of her world. She rejected the silhouettes and the figures. Her eyes withdrew; she heard them fall deep in her head. Water rippled secretly into her ears.

Mazvita unfolded the baby from the towel. She unwound the towel from her back, peeled it off the back of the child. Mazvita let the towel drop softly, behind her, to the ground. The towel was dirty. It was soggy with the heat. Mazvita circled the baby with her arms, and held him down. She bent slowly forward and the baby moved slightly along her waist, towards her left. She bent further forward and prepared to receive the baby from beneath her arm, under her left shoulder. Mazvita felt the baby in her armpit. She gasped. She waited.

Wings beat past, and rested. Mazvita was startled. The bird rose, disappeared beneath the wreckage. Mazvita lingered with closed eyes, her heart pounding, her elbows pinned to her sides, over the quiet legs of the baby. She searched the end of the alley and again saw the people pass by, in rapid dots, in specks of memory. Knees trembled and bent towards the ground. Mazvita held her muscles tightly, firmly, urgently. The baby grew heavy on her back. Mazvita bowed, yielded to the searing pain. She waited. Mazvita heard a faint murmur move from herself to the baby. She told the baby to keep still. She turned to her right, slid the baby gently but quickly into her waiting hands, in the front. Her hands waited eagerly for her baby. She felt the baby fall in a lump into her hands. Mazvita tightened her eyes. The moment was rich, it filled her arms. The baby fell from her back and rested across her stomach, its legs spread rigidly around her waist. Mazvita raised her back and opened her eyes wide. She saw the baby.

She looked at the top of the child's head. She dipped a sole finger into her mouth then passed it gently over the child. She rested her finger shakingly on the child and remembered. The past came to her in rapid waves that made her heave the child forward, away from her, in a deep and uncontrollable motion of rejection. Her arms shook and she held the child still, like flame. She returned the baby slowly to her stomach and touched again the child's head with a wet finger. She pressed gently the top of the child's head, murmured softly, cooingly. She whispered the child to close its eyes, whispered in an elegant dying lullaby, then she crumbled suddenly to the unwelcoming ground. Mazvita fell hard on the ground. Knees collapsed but she held tightly to the baby, pulling it close to her breast. She fell backward into the mounds of filth and decay and stale water. The moment filled her arms and she held tightly. Pigeons clamoured out of their enclaves. Mazvita clutched the baby, cried steadily, silently, curled her legs inward.

She took the baby and placed it gently into her waiting leg, amid the drifting papers and echoes of ululating wings. Armpits sweltered, pulsating sadly. Mazvita was truly alone.

She held the baby over her leg. She raised her bent knee high, away from the ground. The bottom of her leg, her ankle, supported the rest of the child. The child's body curved inward, as though its back was broken. Mazvita opened the apron wide. She carefully spread the apron over the crook of her right leg. She performed the task deliberately, lingering over each motion, smoothing the cloth into a shiny evenness. It was warm and sweaty within her leg. She felt the sweat grow stickily over her skin. She was grateful. She still breathed, could move forward towards her destination. What did it matter what she suffered?

Where her bent leg met the left, she transferred the baby quietly to the wide spread cloth. She transferred the head of the baby to the white silent apron. The baby lay encased within the embroidered stitching. The baby was sewn up there. She could not do much about the wild stitching though her heart rose against it. She rested the head on the apron, and waited. The child pressed hard on her knee. Mazvita raised her knee gently from the ground and brought the child close to her face. With faintly pleading lips Mazvita felt the forehead of the child.

She gathered her strength in repeated quiet sighs that escaped from her dry lips. Something had sucked the water from the roof of her mouth. It was dry like a pod. She moved her tongue around her mouth, in circles. It felt like a flattened and dried fruit.

She breathed hard, absorbing the stale air in the alley, the sound of rustling paper, of car hooters piercing the darkness. She breathed the poverty and the loneliness, the black walls tarnished and buried with the cries of abandoned dreams, of apparitions of laughter fuelled with desperation, of voices pained. She breathed vigorously the darkness of the alley. She breathed, in an exhilarated effort to secure her own survival, to rise to her feet, to carry the moment solidly in her arms.

Mazvita turned and looked over her shoulder. She turned yet again and looked. She looked. The sound grew thick, made rich the darkness. She swung forward, her head suspended above the child, swung forward. She bent over the child and touched it with her forehead. She swayed far to one side, returned smoothly to the other, above the child. She bent forward, over the head of the child. There was release. She held herself up from the ground. Mazvita braced for the journey.

The silence was temporary. She had to move fast before the harrowing intrusion came back, haunting and persistent, haunting and truly her own. In one pleading effort she raised her neck. Her face jutted angrily forward. She expected not mysterious visitations, no changes to her world. She only pulled her neck high in an effort to detach her head from her body, somehow, to walk around with her body completely severed. Her thoughts would be free. It was the constant nearness of her head to the child that made her frenzied and perplexed. There was not enough space between her and the child she bore on her back. If she could remove her head, and store it a distance from the stillness on her back, then she could begin. She would be two people. She would be many. One of her would be free. One of her would protect the other. She wanted one other of her, that is how she conceived of her escape. She attempted this enigmatic separation by drawing mightily forward, by dropping her chest down, by pulling her arms to the back, by restraining her shoulders. Her neck rose upward and she felt a violent pain delve downward to her back. She looked up.

She looked up and saw a white sky clear and untarnished, beyond the roof tops. The suddenness of the sky surprised her. The whiteness folded into the alley, squeezed down over the rooftops, near and white. She welcomed the sky. The brightness broke into her eyes. It was a fervent cloud and it lingered. Mazvita did not hurry. She kept the moment for as long as she could. She felt light. She felt lifted from the darkness, light, out of the darkness. The cloud fell downward, very near to her, then it passed, uncovering a grey and torpid roof. Her eyes were vivid with tears. Her head sank down, down. The sky grew pale. She turned back to the baby and lifted it up, together with the apron. She lifted the baby up above her head, and freed her legs. She freed her legs upward, forward, straight. She uncurled her back and stood upright, she bent forward, she slid the baby's head and the apron over her left shoulder onto her waiting back. Her back shivered, not with cold. A tremendous unbearable ripple. She felt the baby settle familiarly over her back. Yesterday frightened her with its familiarity.

She felt the baby's head beneath her neck, and she moved her body briefly, to centre the baby along her frame. The baby settled on her back. She pulled the stiff legs of the baby, resting them along her twisted waist, and tucked the apron beneath the baby, then she pulled the bottom ends of the apron tight against her stomach, pulled the top down, and the two sets of strings met in the middle of her breasts. She tied the bands together. She made a tight knot that threatened to sever her across the middle. She tore hard into her breasts with the apron bands.

The apron pulled hard at her neck, strangled her last breath. She continued to tighten the knot, though the bands were already shortened, and no further movement could be secured. She pulled at the stillness, hard. The stillness made her pause in her pulling, and she listened to it. The stillness made her entire body tremble but she nurtured that stillness because it was hers. She held long and patiently. The cloth tore at her skin, into her palm. She did not protest the pain. She preferred that continuous strangling. It kept her awake, the suffocation, it kept her alive and desperate. She tightened the firm bands, and recovered herself from the debris, from the shelter and secrecy.

She searched the ground in furtive glances, with a twisted and narrowed brow, with shaking limbs. She moved forward though the air held her in a ferocious grip. Her back tightened, and she moved forward, away from the narrow passage. Mazvita moved forward.

Milk poured from her breasts. It fell in soured lumps.

∞∞

6

"Nyenyedzi," she whispered and he looked towards her.

She recognized his back though he wore the bright green overalls, like all the other men in the tobacco barn. It was a busy place. The bales of tobacco arrived early in the morning in long trucks and the workers carried them into the shed. They held their arms forward. They heaved. They moved forward. The bales sat in sections marked throughout the hall, in high piles taller than the men. There was a strong smell of decay throughout. It was dark and damp inside where the leaves were tied together with rope, tied tightly together. The thick rope cut through the thickened leaves and the leaves bulged in angry circles. The leaves swelled outward, away from the rope.

At the end of the day Mazvita felt weak, felt faint and frantic from the tobacco smell which spread towards her, like decay. The tobacco rose from inside her. The air was mouldy. Dark and wet. She turned her eyes towards the asbestos roof where the air hung downward like soot. It choked her, that smell. Out of the shed, she breathed slowly and preciously.

The storehouse was not far from the farm itself. She had worked on the farm, but now she made tea in a little kitchen behind the storehouse for the foreman and his assistants. She missed the bright open fields where she had worked, but now she was closer to Nyenyedzi, she did not mind the dark. It was dark in the shed.

The bales lit the place with a decaying glow, with the strong biting scent. She looked forward to the end of the day when they left the shed and walked through the forest to the edge of the farm, to the huts. Nyenyedzi walked with her. She feared the forest, and the war. Nyenyedzi did not mind taking her into the forest, after work. He had no fear of the war.

"Why did you leave your home?" he asked. "You are not from Kadoma."

"I needed work. I heard there is always work on the tobacco farms. I am from Mubaira, in Mhondoro."

"We must go back together to Mubaira."

"I can never go back there."

"Why?"

"The war is bad in Mhondoro. It is hard to close your eyes there and sleep. It is hard to be living. I left because I want to reach the city. I cannot return so quickly."

"We must go back. I want to meet your parents."

"It is kind of you, Nyenyedzi, but it is hard to find words for certain things. I really must go to the city. One day I woke up in a mist, you know, the kind you enter with your shoulders. The morning seemed to rise from the ground, because the mist was so thick and spread slowly from the ground. Even the sun turns white at dawn, in that mist. My arms were heavy as I walked in that early morning to carry water from the river. I only had my arms, because my legs were buried in the mist, but I felt the mist moving upward, towards my face. It was strange to walk separated like that. Then I felt something pulling me down into the grass. This something pulled hard at my legs, till I fell down. I saw nothing, because the mist was so heavy. I tumbled through that mist, screaming into the grass. I had forgotten about my legs. It was a man that pulled me into that grass. He held a gun. I felt the gun, though I did not see it. After that experience, I decided to leave."

They walked on, silently, along the path.

"We should live together and cook together," Nyenyedzi said suddenly. "This is a good place for us to live."

"I cannot live here. We must go to the city and live there. I don't know if we are safe even in this place. The war is everywhere. We must go to the city. It is said there is no war there. Freedom has already arrived. Do you see the people who come from the city... they have no fear in their eyes. Look at how frightened we are here. Can freedom arrive here the way it has arrived in the city?"

"In a big place like that. We will be lost. We will even lose one another."

"No. It is the perfect place to begin. It is better there than here. Harari. The news about the freedom in that city has reached all the ears in Mubaira. I am waiting to make enough money, then I will go on the bus. It will be easier in Harari. You can forget anything in the city."

"You can forget your own mother. I cannot go to Harari. I like the land. I cannot leave the land and go to a strange unwelcoming place. I have heard terrible stories about Harari. Everyone carries a knife there. A knife that you can fold and place in your pocket. A knife that you can open quickly when you are in trouble. Imagine a place with such a knife. Then there are those robbers called *skuz'apo*. They empty your pockets before you can blink. They take a knife from your own pocket and kill you with it. You cannot even trust your shadow in a place like that. Some people have robbed and killed their own parents in that place. What kind of a place is that?"

"I have to see this with my own eyes. I am going there Nyenyedzi."

"No. I cannot go there. I have worked here for two years now, and I know this place better than you do. I was born not far from here. You have not lived here long and say you are leaving. If you stayed a year we could make decisions. We could go to Mubaira first and meet your parents. The city will bury us."

"I must move on. I will move on."

Mazvita carried a strong desire to free herself from the burden of fear, from the skies licked with blue and burning with flame. She had not told Nyenyedzi everything. She had not told him about what that man who pulled her down had whispered to her, how she ran through the mist with torn clothes, with his whispering carried in her ears, how the sky behind her exploded as the village beyond the river burnt, and she shouted loud because her arms reached forward, but not forward enough to rescue the people, to put out the flame, and she cried and ran with her two legs missing, buried, and she thought she ran with her arms because she saw them swing forward, swing back, swing forward, carry her through that mist towards the huts which mingled with the river and her crying, then she fell down, looked beneath the mist at the burning hut because the mist had lifted, now formed a canopy over her head, and she discovered her legs, whole, beneath her body, and she discovered a large circle of bright yellow sun. Waiting, burning, naturally.

∞∞

7

Harari.

Newspaper headings covered the dark alley, promised no freedom to the agitated people. But there were ample signs of the freedom the people had already claimed for themselves – empty shells of Ambi, green and red. The world promised a lighter skin, greater freedom. It was 1977, freedom was skin deep but joyous and tantalising. *Ambi*. Freedom was coy and brash, spread between palms, shared and physical. Freedom was a translucent nose, ready to drop. Freedom left one with black-skinned ears. A mask. A carnival. Reality had found a double, turbulent and final. Freedom spoke from behind a mask, but no one asked any deep questions, no one understood what freedom truly was. To be sure, it was boisterous. Ambi would do for now, certainly. No one questioned the gaps in reality. If there was a gap anywhere, there was an opening too. Freedom was any kind of opening through which one could squeeze. People fought to achieve gaps in their reality. The people danced in an enviable kind of self-mutilation.

Freedom squeezed out of a tube was better than nothing, freedom was, after all, purchasable. It was sensual, and that was to be longed for, procured even if the cost was nothing less than one's soul. Such negotiations were easy. It was risky to carry a soul in the the city streets, as Mazvita had discovered. In Harari, it was best to sell your soul to the first and easiest bidder. In this one case of the *Ambi Generation* at least one received a permanent mark for the exchange, an elaborate transformation.

Skin fell to the ground.

The people had been efficient accomplices to the skinning of their faces, to the unusual ritual of their disinheritance. They were skinned like goats before a ritual conceived to bring back the dead, that is, with happy song. They had lain in rows in the searing sun while their skin fell from their faces, pulled and pulled away. It was clear that is how the process had been executed for their faces were perpetually astonished. It is like that with skins that are put out to dry. The people walked the streets without any faces, invisible, like ghosts. Was it a surprise then that they could not recognize one another? Ancestors dared not recognize them. The people had found such a breath-stopping freedom the ancestors knew them not, dared not know them. Faces dried under troubled rays. The people stopped in amazement, greeted each other, swept on. On the other side of the streets their skins burnt an ill and silenced song. The streets smelt of burning skin. *Nyore Nyore*. It was like that in 1977.

∞∞

8

The silence cleansed her.

Mazvita gathered the whispering he had spread between her legs, over her arms, over her face. She ran far into the mist but the whispering, a frightful memory, encompassed her. She gathered the whispering into a silence that she held tightly within her body. She sheltered in the silence. The silence was hers, though he had initiated it. The silence was a quietness in her body, a deafness to the whispering that escaped from the lips of the stranger. He had claimed her, told her that she could not hide the things of her body, that she must bring a calabash of water within her arms, and he would drink. He had tired of drinking from the river. She must offer him water with cupped hands. She must kneel so that he could drink. He whispered as though he offered her life, in gentle murmuring tones, unhurried, but she felt his arms linger too long over her thighs, linger searchingly and cruelly, and she knew that if there was life offered between them, it was from herself to him – not offered, but taken.

The silence was a treasure. Mazvita felt a quietness creep from the earth into her body as he rested above her, spreading his whispered longing over her. She had slept very still, but briefly, before she started to run. She ran with the slipperiness pouring between her thighs, except she was not aware that her legs were still hers. She was aware, simply, that somewhere her skin carried a terrible wetness that she needed to defeat. Mazvita longed for a silence without a ripple or an echo in it.

He reached for her back and she lay motionless, unaware that she still had a name that was hers. She had discovered the silence to keep his breathing from her back. *Hanzvadzi...* he said. You are my sister... he whispered. He did not shout or raise his voice but invited her to lie still in a hushed but serious rhythm. His voice was monotonous, low, but firmly held in his mouth, in his arms. He spoke in a tone trained to be understood, not heard. Mazvita fought to silence his whispering. The task nearly killed her. It was difficult to find all his whispered words. She could not always recognize all the words, and when she did, her effort was to quickly gather them into that distance she had prepared inside of her. She longed deeply for the silence to be complete. She longed to escape the insistent cries of his triumph.

The silence was not a forgetting, but a beginning. She would grow from the silence he had brought to her. Her longing for growth was deep, and came from the parts of her body he had claimed for himself, which he had claimed against all her resistance and her tears. So she held her body tight to close him out, to keep the parts of her body that still belonged to her, to keep them near to herself, recognizable and near. She allowed her arms to move forward, ahead of her, and she ran through the mist, following her arms. She welcomed the stillness the silence brought to her body. It made her thoughts coherent, brought calm to her face. Mazvita was strong.

The tightness brought to her a complete silence, of her womanhood. She fought hard for the silence long after that morning. The days grew into months. The moon glowed a thin but silent awaiting. Mazvita had lost her seasons of motherhood. She did not question this dryness of her body but welcomed it as a beginning, a clear focus of her emotion, a protecting impulse. She was pure and strong and whole. She recovered her name. Mazvita. She sheltered in the barrenness and the silence of her name. She had discovered a redeeming silence. Mazvita.

Mazvita accepted the season of emptiness as her own particular fate. She grew from the emptiness. The emptiness lifted her from the ground and she felt something like power, like joy, move through her. The heaviness lifted from her shoulders and her arms, from her eyes which she had closed after the mist had collapsed into her eyes. Mazvita wished for an emotion as perfectly shaped as hate, harmful as sorrow, but she had not seen the man's face. She could not find his face, bring it close enough to attach this emotion to it. Hate required a face against which it could be flung but searching for the face was futile. Instead, she transferred the hate to the moment itself, to the morning, to the land, to the dew-covered grass that she had felt graze tenderly against her naked elbow in that horrible moment of his approach, transferred it to the prolonged forlorn call of the strange bird she heard cry a shrill cry in the distance, so shrill and loud that she had had to suppress her own cry which had risen to her lips. The unknown bird had silenced her when she needed to tell of her own suffering, to tell not to someone else – certainly not to the man – but to hear her own suffering uttered, acknowledged, within that unalterable encounter. A cry, her own cry, would have been a release of all the things she had lost. But she did not cry then and so it was as if she had lost the world. And all the many things that contained this loss, continued to remind her of her pain. She transferred the hate to the something that she could see, that had shape and colour and distance. The mist had taught her that morning is not always birth.

Mazvita felt the man breathe eagerly above her. She hated the breathing; she hated even more the longing in the breathing; mostly, she hated the land that pressed beneath her back as the man moved impatiently above her, into her, past her. Mazvita sought the emptiness of her body. Afterwards, she did not connect this emptiness to the man because she thought of him not from inside her, but from outside. He had never been inside her. She connected him only to the land. It was the land that had come towards her. He had grown from the land. She saw him grow from the land, from the mist, from the river. The land had allowed the man to grow from itself into her body.

Mazvita gathered the silence from the land into her body.

∞∞

9

"The land belongs to our feet because only they can carry the land. It is only our feet which own the land. Our hands can only carry clods of earth at a time. We cannot carry the land on our shoulders. No one can take the land away. To move away from the land is to admit that it has been taken. It is to abandon it. We have to wait here. We have to wait here with the land, if we are to be loyal to it, and to those who have given it to us. The land does not belong to us. We keep the land for the departed. That is why we can work on the land while strangers believe it can belong only to them. How can something so vast and mysterious belong to anybody? Only that which we can carry between our fingers can belong to us. No one can own the land. Because this is true we are fighting the strangers so that they leave, and we can protect the land. They have told us it is not right for us to protect the land, yet they have asked us to work on it. Have you seen them working on the land as we do? They are strangers to the land. Our feet own the land much more than the claims of their mouths, much more than the claims of their fingers. The land recognizes only those who work upon it. It knows our breath and our sweat."

Nyenyedzi spoke with a brightness on his face, a glow unhidden. He would not leave the land. But Mazvita did not agree with the vision he held for the land. She had no fear of departures. She was restless, though she admired and cared for this man. She turned away from him. She held a heaviness in her mouth that Nyenyedzi failed to fathom.

"We are servants paid poorly for our labours. We cannot decide which crop to grow, or when to grow it. We do not pray for the success of our crop because it is no longer our crop. We cannot pray for another's crop. There are no rituals of harvest, of planting the crop into the ground. We labour because it is our task to labour. We do not own the land. The land is enclosed in barbed fences, and we sleep amid the thorn bushes, in the barren part of the land. We live in fear because even those who fight in our name threaten our lives."

"It is like that with a war. We must remain here or else join the fight, fight to cleanse the land, not find new dreams to replace our ancient claim."

"The land has forgotten us. Perhaps it dreams new dreams for itself."

"You lack patience and hope, Mazvita, you want things to belong to you, just like the stranger does. You want to possess, to hold things between your hands and say they belong to you. You do not see that things belong to you not because you have held them, but because they have held you. It is like that with the land. It holds and claims you. The land is inescapable. It is everything. Without the land there is no day or night, there is no dream. The land defines our unities. There is no prayer that reaches our ancestors without blessing from the land. Land is birth and death. If we agree that the land has forgotten us, then we agree to be dead."

"What you say about the land is true, but does this truth belong equally to all of us?"

"The truth does not belong to anyone. It is our truth."

"Truth changes like a sky. The strangers have taken the land. They have grown tobacco where we once buried the dead. The dead remain silent. They have grown tobacco where we once worshipped and prayed. The land has not rejected them. They have harvested much crop. I remember..."

"They have not grown the crop. We have grown the crop. The land has yielded to our hand. They will leave the land. We are fighting them."

"We wait ... we wait for a new death ... for the death of the land."

"The land has claimed us for its truth."

"I remember ..."

Mazvita understood that Nyenyedzi would not agree to leave, that he would wait here, or else join the fight. Either way he did not belong to her. She wanted something different for her truth. She wanted to conquer her reality then, and not endure the suspension of time. She felt a strong sense of her own power and authority, of her ability to influence and change definitions of her own reality, adjust boundaries to her vision, banish limits to her progress. She felt supreme with every moment. She had left Mubaira because it suited her to move forward. She possessed a strong desire for her liberty, and did not want to linger hopelessly between one vision and the next. She had loved the land, saw it through passionate and intense moments of freedom, but to her the land had no fixed loyalties. She gathered from it her freedom which it delivered to her wholly and specially. If it yielded crop, then it could also free her, like the plants which grew upon it and let off their own blooms, their own scents, their own colour, while anchored on the land. She felt free like a seed released from one of such plants. She could grow anywhere. Mazvita felt buoyant. Her relationship to the land involved such buoyant freedoms. She had the potential to begin again. Hope mingled with desire. Mazvita was ambitious. She wanted to discover something new in her world. She understood the kind of loyalty Nyenyedzi referred to, but she was ready to move into another sphere of presence, to depart. She did not care for certainties, each moment would uncover its secret, but she would be there, ahead of that moment, far ahead. She moved close to Nyenyedzi, and touched him. Mazvita had no fear of departures.

10

A violent wind carried Mazvita forward.

No one noticed or remembered her. Mazvita was sure of her direction so she started to walk. Her footsteps were jerky and faltering. She walked. She walked sideways, because her left shoulder leaned forward. It was her broken side. Her bones spread in splintered fragments, across her back. She leaned farther sideways and felt, once more, her bones fall against each other. Her bones built a mountain on her back.

Mazvita. Her back was broken.

It was hard to support the child when her back was so much broken, but she tried, and she tried to walk quickly through the crowds. It was hard work. Harari was busy and indifferent.

Mazvita. Her eyes were unseeing. They simply led her forward. She had surrendered her sight when she heard the violent breaking on her back. She had relieved herself of sight because it was easier to be blind and still journey forward. She had surrendered her own eyes because it suited her to do so. The ritual was fulfilling and complete. She lost all capacity for dream. She felt less burdened, less susceptible to injury. After all she had injured herself irreparably, she could not hurt beyond the hurting so hurtful.

Empty and abandoned, she walked, leaning forward, past caring.

The city pushed forward. It was 1977. It was nothing to see a woman with a blind stare on her face, with a baby fixed spidery on her back. It was nothing to be sorrowful. The city was like that. There was a uniformity about suffering, a wisdom about securing your own kind of suffering, your own version of going forward. The idea was to go forward, even those who had died in the streets knew that, they crawled towards the alleys.

Death, properly executed, could be mistaken for progress.

∞∞

11

Cloth ripped downward, and the children ran with naked shoulders towards their mothers. They crept beneath the barbed wire and rose from the ground to nurse their bruised ankles.

The building sat in a mud row on the edge of the barbed wire. Two parallel walls of mud and poles had been built then subdivided to form tight cramped residences for the workers. On one side low entrances were carved into the wall. The place was grass thatched. The grass hung low behind the huts, left gaps that allowed the smoke to escape, allowed the sun to enter freely, allowed the rain. Often the men retrieved wide plastic bags once used to cover the tobacco when it was carried to the city, and they tied these over the holes. The thatching was made of intermittent marriages of plastic and grass. A row could contain up to six dwellings. There was no land granted to build well spaced huts.

From the entrance, which was black with smoke, Nyenyedzi watched Mazvita kneel beside the fire preparing the evening meal. She felt him standing there because the slice of light which had been illuminating the room had vanished. He remained quiet. He entered in slow guarded footsteps and sat at the opposite side of the fire.

"Can I get more wood for you?" he asked. His asking was richly coated, longing. The bag she had already packed was hidden in the recesses of the room, pushed under the blankets folded among the utensils, among the things they had shared, before sharing this. She felt their heavy parting. She blew hard at the fire, and paused. She held her breath as it moved upward. She held her breath there where her chest was pushed outward. She held the moment of their sharing in her mouth. She paused. She released her breath, gathered softly, from her mouth, from deep in her stomach. Her head dropped down.

"I did not see that you had arrived. The food is almost ready." She rose, turned backward, retrieved a vessel filled with water. Nyenyedzi rose, bent beneath the door way, passed through, then stood outside. He waited for her.

She followed Nyenyedzi with the water in the basin. He held both hands out and she poured the water over him. He rubbed his hands together, and washed them. She paused as he rubbed the dirt from his fingers. She watched him dig beneath his nails, search deep into the crevices. His nails were wide and flat and cracked, black with the soil. He held out his hands and she poured the water over them. The water fell to the ground, splashed onto her bare feet. She allowed the water to descend, gently, over his hands.

She handed him the basin, now half full with the water, and he poured the water over her hands. She washed her hands rapidly and nervously. He poured the water very deliberately over her hands. She grew anxious through his pleading. The water fell over her bare arms and ran over the back of her hands. She turned her hands and received the water which brought the setting sun in drops, to her fingers. She extended her arms and held her hands away from her body. She washed her hands and thanked him. She retrieved the basin from him, empty, and turned to enter the unlit room that they had shared. He followed cautiously behind her. The fire was dying.

"Mazvita," he called, as she entered. She stood still. She could hardly bear it. The stillness was theirs. It was heavy.

"The land... we cannot forget it, it cannot forget us," Nyenyedzi muttered.

She served the food and they ate, held in silence, in their fears, their desires. He pleaded.

Mazvita fought with each gesture of her hand, with her eyebrows raised and searching, with her feet held beneath her body, shoulders raised, a forehead tired and wet, toes patiently curled, her back leaning away from him.

He held a pleading desperate gaze. He called upon the land to give to him this woman that he cared for. He could not leave the land, and be a man. He was afraid of returning and not knowing the land, of the land not knowing him. He feared untried absences. He preferred the histories of his people.

The woman rose above the land and scorned its slow promises, its intermittent loyalties. She had such a will, and he knew that he could not equal her passion for beginnings. He heard her fight, heard her defeat him, in that silence. He raised his head from the plate of food, and met her. The woman confronted the land with her passion for escape.

"Mazvita," he called.

Mazvita carried a bold frantic gaze that Nyenyedzi failed to recognize. They were free, finally, of each other's desires.

∞∞

12

Mazvita could no longer remember the woman who had sold her the apron. *Amai.* She remembered that. *Amai.* She was indeed a mother. It was heavy to be a mother. It made one recognizable in the streets, even when one no longer recognized oneself. *Amai.* It was painful. *Amai.* The seller's voice followed her through the crowds, but it no longer referred to her. *Amai.* It referred to any woman who passed by, who carried a baby on her back, who was a potential mother. *Amai.* It had never referred to her, that *Amai*, at least not specifically. She had adopted the woman's voice for her truth. It was not enough. *Amai* referred only to her silver coins. Mazvita was alone.

The white apron spread across her back like a skinned animal. The baby rested within it, its head folded down. The head was heavy. Mazvita felt the head grow heavy on her back. She wiped her face with a lonely naked arm, then spread her hands cupped to her back, circling the baby. Her hands met, joined, behind her back. Her palms grew warm. Mazvita buried the baby in her arms. Mazvita had tucked some of the baby's clothes along the sides of the apron where there were pockets of empty space, above the baby's knees where its legs attempted to curve around her waist.

It was the two bottom ends of the apron that she felt cut through her waist. She had gathered the endless lengths of stitched apron bands and tied them firmly. She had tied the bands to fight the weight of the child. Mazvita buried the baby on her back.

Mazvita repeatedly formed an incredibly tight knot, then a short while later she would untie the bands, and start all over again, convinced that the knot was not firm enough, that the baby might fall out, that someone might pause long enough to look into her secret. She harnessed all her strength, all her memories. Each grew threateningly faint. Untying the bands was not easy, but she fought the knot. She bit dangerously, her neck pulled forward, her shoulders peaks of anguish.

Mazvita was in a fierce protracted battle with the apron, tying it, untying it, tying it. With each secured moment of her untying, she bent her back forward, leaned towards the ground, and felt the baby slide forward towards her neck, slide forward. A silent sliding, and her neck shrunk with cold. Her head fell backward, towards the baby.

Her head met that of the baby in a soft loving collision. It was growing soft that head pressed on her back. Soft. She panicked at the thought but the thought pressed hard beneath her armpits, and she felt a sweat break freely there, flow in ripples of salty tears. The air was stale and hot, it was not to be trusted, and the baby was so heavily wrapped. The air hung over the ears with a promise of fatality.

She touched what she thought was the baby's forehead with the back of her head, and felt consoled. The baby felt hard. Her knees trembled and sank downward. Mazvita. She remembered at least her own name and sang it to her baby. She sang deep and slow. She sang deep deep, from her insides to her baby, a lullaby that came from the recesses of an ancient memory. The tune was familiar, but coarse, it seemed ground from between two violent stones. It was a tune for grinding corn, not for awakening tenderness. Mazvita, she sang. She polished her song into a rhythmic but futile

-41-

undertaking. She sang with arms spread wide in a spontaneous greeting of the earth, a weeping farewell. Her arms were heavy with the child, remembered. She spread her arms wide like the sky.

It was a song lyrical and free. She sent a song from her back to the waiting child, fed the baby with that song, with her name. The song was the only thing that belonged to her and that she could still remember, that made any kind of sense to her for the future held her fate in disarray. She could offer the song. She was desperate and lost. A song was a kind of freedom, a promise of birth and beginnings. Dear was that name she fed to her child, a ululating symphony, a melody enchanting and lonesome. She sang with the last breath in her body for she was certain there would be no life for her after this. It was not possible that she would be buried and then live. She had died a final death.

Mazvita did not know if she was going to Mubaira or Kadoma. Both destinations seemed necessary and certain. She had arrived here. She had arrived there. She knew nothing of arrivals, only departures. She knew about departures because she had mistaken them for beginnings. Departures were not beginnings, they were resolutions, perhaps, they were acts of courage, perhaps. Futile illusions had marked her departures. Birth, for her, had not been a beginning, but a newer kind of departure, an entrapment rare and nullifying. She had tired of departures. Mazvita tried to imagine that there was a beginning even in this sorrowful finality. It seemed the end had always been there, had always waited.

She could decide on the bus, about her destination. It did not matter, because the destination was only another place in her journey. She saw herself unanchored, moving forward, always moving forward, with the weight of the baby on her back. She would never rid herself of this particular suffering. The baby was her own, truly her own burden. Now her main concern was to secure a seat on the bus. A part of her said there were beginnings, in both directions. She had a rare chance to choose her beginnings, to undo her past. She might choose the point of birth, or of love. There were inviting dramas in both, passions bright and elegant. She had begun twice in her life, perhaps three times, perhaps such a number of times there was really no use counting, for what was it to begin?

Mazvita knew about waterfalls because she had found herself on the edge of a cliff. She had not known there were such rugged and desperate spaces in which one could continue to live, even though a massive river tumbled over one's head, and stones followed, and boulders beat against the shoulders, and one screamed and screamed. One could live in such uninhabitable places.

Mazvita felt herself tumble and fall but there was no ground beneath, only an interminable echo which she followed with her body while it spiralled into a darkness loud and indifferent. She had not fallen like that, because she held herself against the hard ground, pushed her right palm down, and rose awkwardly. She steadied herself, and moved on. She still heard the echo that she had followed, and mistrusted it. One side of her arm, on which she had fallen, was covered in dust. Her face was bruised. She passed a dry tongue over her cracked upper lip. There were parts of herself she dared not trust. The truths her imagination asserted formed a major part of her distrust, of her hopelessness. She trusted only the cold weight on her back – the toes small, curled and cold. She straightened her back. She stood still.

Mazvita held onto the baby and the apron and the last strands of sanity, to propel her steadily forward, for she carried such a weight on her back. She untied the apron string once more, cautiously but quickly. And as usual, she cast a loud searching glance towards her surroundings. The baby was precious, not like jewels, but like hope finely chiselled. It was like that with the baby.

She untied the apron. She looked frantically around. The pain tore at her back. The betrayal was familiar so she ignored it and went on with her task. Her fingers had mastered an unimaginable dexterity, proportionate to her suffering. Without lifting her head she turned her eyes stealthily to the left, stealthily to the right, then closed them in one unhesitating movement. A scream threatened to escape from her throat. Her throat was constrictred and yet she felt the scream push like a current upwards towards her mounth. She held her eyes tightly closed.

She leaned forward and felt the apron grow loose over her shoulders. It cut her shoulders, the apron. It pierced the place where her arm swung forward, backward. Her arm swung forward ever so loosely, like wet bark hanging on the side of a trunk, freshly peeled. She was surprised that she could still manipulate her arm, bring it forward, pull that last bit of strength from it and transfer it to the knot forming on the apron. How was she to undo that knot but to lie down, and die.

She had lost her freedom. Death was another kind of freedom, and she longed for it. Her death, that is.

She protected a longing deep as death.

∞∞

13

Mazvita did not have to know anyone. Not herself, not anyone. Knowing was a hindrance. It pinned you down. After that you started recognizing people. Recognizing yourself. That was the danger. It was best to remain anonymous. Some things you just can't figure out. Harari was like that. To be here was not to be here at all, that's what made being here. It was special. The absence filled you up. It didn't creep up on you, try to surprise you, gently and anonymously. You walked right into it, hard like a wall. Hard hitting hardness. Concrete and rock hit you on the forehead and if you were lucky it broke your skull, then there was nothing to remember, the absence was total. A new life began, grew around you, embraced you like a hurricane. Sometimes it killed you. That was what was good about absence. Its dependability. Its undoubted ability for harm. People liked that about absence. They had tired of being here, choking on every thought. Thinking was dangerous. Absence more so. They chose the greater danger, arriving unprotected, ready to be injured. That is how naive they were about freedom.

Freedom was round and smooth and yellow, an earthly version of the sun, hand-held. But whoever heard of a hand-held freedom. Yet each sought an egg laid with only them in mind, laid right into their palm, warm, wet, soft.

It was like that when she arrived in the city. She felt a rare freedom eagerly anticipated. It moved over her just like that. The buildings were so high they made her want to crouch, or bury herself in the ground, anything but to walk up straight. She collapsed in a heap on the pavement and watched the cars move past. She sat curled on the cold cement block. Multitudes of feet moved by. Harari was a pestilence. Feet swished past. The city was unapologetic. The city was on time. Harari was festive. Roads were four wheeled, black tarred and moving.

No one cast her a pitiful glance. She was not there at all. Her name was only hers, she could change it at any time. She called herself Rosie while she sat there, and laughed inwardly. She called herself Mildred... then Margaret... then Angelina... then Constance... Juliet. She preferred Julie to Juliet. Mazvita, she would remain. She did not want to remember what Nyenyedzi had called her. A name like that was not for remembering in the midst of such drumming. The city was busy in every direction that she looked, and she looked everywhere.

It was a rare kind of freedom this, to be so busy and purposeful. She wondered what happened to the aged, in this city so determined to be free, for the old tempered movement, tempered dream. The city was a place which hid its old. Perhaps no one ever lived here long enough to be toothless. If you had no teeth here, you had no life. That much was clear. It never occurred to her that the young also died natural deaths.

Feet moved in whirls of free flowing cloth. Men and women wore trousers. REVOLUTION – a small tag along the waist, in black and white. The widened bottom of the trousers turned and turned. It was also an era for turntables and Long Play. Freedom came in circles. Endless and dizzying. What was freedom if it could be curtailed and contained and passed around? Freedom was a thought tantalising and personal. You had to wear your own freedom to be sure it had arrived. 1977. That is how it was expressed. People walked into shops and bought revolutions. If your revolution was white, and wide, then you had circled your dream, made a complete revolution more definite than the sun. There was a satellite to every vision. It was not a year for comets, really, though fire coloured the sky. That fire was the periphery of dream, not the dream itself. The dream was physical, a caress. It circled ankles. Clad into an expanding silhouette, you died in the streets and it did not matter. You could starve to death. Everyone was an over-clad and spearless revolutionary. Magazines showed former slaves with a new gospel of truth and freedom. But here they had not inherited the blood of foraging white masters and therefore worked extra hard to achieve that fine Afro hair. Men heated metal, close-toothed Afro combs and lifted their hair from the scalp, the women, who already knew freedom was purchasable walked into glittering *Ambi* shops and bought their prepared Afro wigs. Thus clad, they asserted an inchoate independence. Independence was memory and style. Black had never been as beautiful as when it married slavery with freedom.

∞∞

14

There were no greetings, preliminaries or rituals to courtship. At least none that Mazvita recognized. The man walked up to her in easy loitering footsteps on the side of the road where she sat. He swung efficiently towards her. She noticed his arm swing forward. He swung his arms in obvious and deliberate motions of liberty. He did not keep still even as he asked her if she needed a place to stay. He had such a look.... It suited her to consider he was being thoroughly helpful. That is how naive she was about his freedom.

He was tall and when he spoke, his voice departed in sudden hissing spurts. His face was round and small, and his mouth was wide. His mouth seemed unsuited to his small face. His teeth were set evenly beneath a small nose. He swung his arm repeatedly towards his nose, and wiped it down. He swung his right arm like this between every sentence, in between his arm hung as if helpless. The gesture made him sympathetic. It was not clear whether he had acquired the gesture to draw attention to his nose or to hide it. It was the same with his legs. They were thin and long and swung forward with each movement. It was possible he had thought of swinging his right leg to wipe his nose. Mazvita stared at him in fascination.

He offered to take her home on his bicycle, his fingers swinging, pointing, from his wrist at the bicycle which waited on the opposite side of the road. He pulled his head towards her, towards the bicycle, back to her. The decision was easy.

Mazvita had never sat on a bicycle before. The thought made her strange, eager and careless. It tantalized her. It seemed inevitable that she should start life in the city with an elaborate undertaking. They moved together towards the bicycle. He swung determinedly ahead. He searched backward to ensure that she followed. His head made a quick backward glance, swept forward. She watched his newness with a fascinated stare. She held her head carefully above her shoulders. The cars screeched to a stop, moved on, screeched again.

He made her sit with both her legs to one side of the road, and when he turned, she had to pull her weight back to regain her support. The whole exercise was free, pleasurable, careless and uncaring. A public display. She was so involved with her particular version of freedom she did not see that no one noticed her. Ornate yellow blooms kept her memory hopeful. Then she turned a corner and met another woman sitting just like her, and she wanted to wave at their mutual freedom. But she needed both hands to hold onto the seat if she was to remain stable, so she hesitated, and in any case, when she looked at the woman, there was no sign of recognition or sharing.

The man took little time to know her. He was agile.

"Joel. I am Joel." He cast a searching hesitating glance at her, then turned to look in the distance.

"Mazvita," she said warmly. She was getting used to this nimble creature. His mouth was wide. She expected him to make elaborate declarations. He was quick with his mouth, with all his moves. Joel.

Joel liked this new girl. She was shy and self-possessed. She would not ask him for money like all those other girls he had gone through. If he had anything to do with it he would keep her here. At least till he tired of her.

Joel was a miracle. He rode through many streets, oblivious of the hooters. He had a quickness in his speech, a quickness in his movements, a quickness everywhere. She did not find these habits suspicious. She simply stared at his quick legs and fingers. His eyes blinked so quickly that it was a miracle he saw anything. Nyenyedzi was not quick like that. The idea of thinking of this man and of Nyenyedzi at the same time made her laugh. This man was like a machine, ready to go somewhere. She wondered if all the men in the city were like this. He did not even ask to touch her but simply took off his clothes, dropped them on the floor, lay down beside her. "Sleep... Sleep," he said afterwards. He was brief. That is how their life together began. There was no discussion, no agreement, no proposal. They just met and stayed together.

It was strange, but it was a freedom divine. Rituals can be inhibiting. Instead, they had a limitless potential to dream, to travel anywhere, if it had occurred to them. In truth, they really could not put the potential to much use. Still, they had a potential and they had claimed it for their truth. Rituals were not livable in Harari, so they forgot about them and created empty spaces in which they wandered aimlessly. It was a torture sometimes, to have so little to care for, but the emptiness was theirs, and it was authentic.

Joel never spoke of consulting her parents concerning living with her like this. Mazvita found herself wondering about it. Though she had told herself this was freedom, it was not easy to forget where she had come from. They lived as though they had no pasts or futures. They lived because they found themselves living, because one was a man, the other a woman, and it was in their nature to need each other. There were no apologies for such spontaneous needs. There were no resolutions or recollections. The present was brimming with ecstasy, with silhouettes of dream. There were no obstacles to their reality. They settled into a life together, in which Joel leapt out of bed in the morning, leapt back in at night. She adjusted to his rhythm. She liked him. He had made Harari easy and reachable for her.

Joel woke in the mist of morning. He never told her where he worked. It was an unnecessary detail. Details were cumbersome. So they stumbled over them, and moved on. They shoved them aside, hid them, burned them, anything but disclosed them. It was better to maintain the strangeness, it kept everything fresh and exciting. Details meant communicating and intimacy. The main point of freedom was maintaining boundaries, though such boundaries were questionable. Mazvita and Joel simply lived together, kept their pasts from each other. It did not matter where they had come from. It did not concern them who had brought them into the world. The city was cramped with discordant sound.

Mazvita became an efficient housekeeper. She ironed Joel's white shirts till they shone. Joel sat on the small bed on weekends in a crisp shirt and paged through *Scope* magazine. Naked white women graced the covers of *Scope*, in tight bikinis. Joel read torn and soiled copies of James Hadley Chase, and grinned marvellously. One day he read a copy of *The Way the Cookie Crumbles* and made love to her on the floor. It was so very quick. She wondered what was in that Hadley Chase. He held her head in the crook of his arm, and read.

∞∞

15

The bus was full of people. They jostled and found seats on which to settle
and exchange greetings. Greetings that were mere affirmations of direction.

"Are you going to Mubaira?"

"Yes, I am going to Mubaira, and you?"

"Yes. I am going to Mubaira. My wife is waiting for me there. It is our
home because my wife is there. She plants the crops."

"I work in the city too. My wife also plants the crops. The city is only
for the money we get. I cannot let my wife join me. The city is corrupt. A
serious woman will not manage to live there. A woman can lose her head.
Only a man can manage those streets, those lights, those policemen. It is
terrible there. If you marry a woman from the city you will have made a
fire and sat on it. She will even tell you to cook. She will ask you to help
unbutton her bra. What kind of a thing is that? I prefer a woman whose
breasts are free and waiting. Take me home now now... the women say to a
man who is passing by... the women swing with their hips, swing arms
covered in plastic bangles. Women's legs are nylon and high. Heels do not
touch the ground. Handbags swing across arms, cross the streets. 1977.
There is a scorpion beneath every rock. The city makes a man frenzied and

hot. The freedom in that city! My wife stays at home, we had a large harvest of groundnuts last year. A whole ten sacks. I wonder how she did it, but a woman's strength is not to be frowned upon."

"It is not the woman. It is the rain. There was a lot of rain last year. All the women had to do was merely harvest."

"Harvesting is work,"

"Yes. It is a woman's work. A woman's back is strong. A man cannot bend like that all day. A man cannot bend like a woman."

"And carry a baby on her back too. A woman's back is made for work. A woman's back is strong as stone."

"The bus is full. It is such a hot day. I don't know if it will rain this year as it did last year. The earth has changed. Whoever heard of such heat. A heat like this brings death."

"Such heat brings rain. It never comes alone. It brings good crops. When the earth is thirsty like this, the rain finally falls in torrents. It shall rain so much we must make ready the thatching of our huts or we shall be left sitting in a clearing."

"A woman's back can perform miracles. We had such a large harvest of groundnuts. Then there was the maize, I cannot even begin to tell you about that. The maize filled four large granaries. If the rain does not fall this year, we shall be safe for another three years, at least."

"We harvested a lot too. But I am certain this heat means rain. I plan to sell all the harvested crop and buy a plough, then we shall really prepare the fields for a harvest to humble all harvests. I am certain of it. This heat brings rain."

The conductor ducked between the many heads, between the two men who shared a seat and talked. The conductor ducked among the heads clad in shining bright scarves which were tied in small loose knots at the back of the women's heads. The scarves were damp along those edges, and carried large smudges of wetness at the top. It was hot on the bus. The women had freed their babies from the back and held them. Most of the babies slept.

The conductor handed tickets out, received some money. He carried a black leather bag bound tightly around his waist, it bounced with his every agile movement. He was rather like an excited locust lost in tall grasses. He could ferret out a passenger who had not paid, without any effort at all. He held his nose pinched into a mole which he kept safe between his eyes, then he turned his head sideways, very quickly. The leather purse was a constant reminder of his importance. His forehead hid beneath a massive fall of thick black hair. He pulled his arm back, shoved it into his leather purse, picked out several coins, leapt forward. His neck jerked sideways. He darted past Mazvita, though she had not paid.

Mazvita saw him move past her. She watched him disappear among the mounds of tied boxes blocking the path to the back. He surfaced, beyond the obstructions, over the large box tightly tied with a black elastic band.

∞∞

16

Mazvita arrived in Harari ready to claim her freedom. Here, she was protected from the hills and the land. Harari banished memory, encouraged hope. Mazvita had a strong desire to grow. She trusted the future and her growth and her desire. She had faith in untried realities because she trusted her own power for change, for adaptation. She welcomed each day with a strong sense of her desire, of her ability to begin, of her belonging. Mazvita had a profound belief in her own reality, in the transformation new geographies promised and allowed, that Harari's particular strangeness released and encouraged. Mazvita recognized Harari as the limitless place in which to dream, and to escape.

Mazvita drew on her own capacity for release which had led her here. She was not frivolous in her ambition. She hoped only not to be harmed by the compromises she had found unavoidable. Joel was inevitable to her existence.

Mazvita was oppressed by her desire for time. She knew that this awareness did not coincide with Harari as she encountered it. Harari challenged the demarcations between day and night, offered distances from time, for part of being here was the forgetting of boundaries to days, of challenging futures. In Harari, years could go by and it would be as though one had arrived only yesterday. The discoveries offered by the city were tempting and endless... The city was contemptuous, it asked, did you only arrive yesterday? Sleep and slowness were denied to those who were of the city. There was no room for sleep because one day led into another without pause, and when you had been in it long enough, you did not make the kind of mistakes that exposed your failure to flow with its time. However, what was it to be here long enough when truly there was no clear measure of time?

Time was precious. Mazvita was caught up in this whirl of time, of freed existence, yet those first days with Joel still weighed heavy on her, because she needed time to secure her freedom. She felt that each day she was without employment drew her closer to Joel and emphasized her dependability. She hoped to recover the time she had spent with Joel because she needed it for herself, for her own growth. She did not share in the belief that time was continuous and endless, that what she had not accomplished today was easily recoverable. She had not banished the future in the way that people in the city had done. It made her frantic and restless to think of the future.

She felt tired, as though she fought against a strong current that determined to move against her. The future threatened her, it was large. She did not want to fall emptily into the future. She did not want to be surprised by it so she worked hard to prepare for each moment before the moment found her. She hid when she could. Time moved on and drew her from her hiding. Mazvita longed for a future in which she would look backwards and feel fulfillment, so her divisions of time were cautious and laboured.

She hoped to succeed. Success could only be measured by holding the past against the future. While Harari set a pace for her existence Mazvita located herself beyond the moment. Mazvita had tired of postponements to her vision. She tried to understand the ceaseless yet inviting ambivalences that defined the city. Mazvita weighed carefully the city's offerings and denials, its testimonies and silences.

At night yellow and white lights mingled and burnt and the sight spread, in the distance, a prophecy of their liberation. It did not matter that they lived in the darkness, with no such lights. It mattered only that they lived close to this spectacular vision, to this vibrating light. The city proposed luminous aspirations. Mazvita felt immediately that there was something to be hoped for in this nearness to the city. Fear attached to her arrival, but the fear was exciting, because it offered release. Mazvita allowed herself to hope. Joel was only another version of the city, an aspect of her potential freedom.

She had met Joel. She liked Joel. She lived with Joel. Joel was not Nyenyedzi, and she had left Nyenyedzi. She did not dream dreams around Joel. She dreamt dreams around herself. In Harari, however, Joel was necessary to her dream. Part of her Harari was Joel. Joel made Harari accessible. The city included Joel.

Mazvita knew that Joel was part of a definition of Harari that she had not anticipated. She had not anticipated the city in its entirety. There were more compromises to be made than she had thought. She looked for work while Joel was away. Mazvita quickly saw that Joel had his own version of the city, and that he was weaving her into it. She would not succumb to being a mere aspect of his dream.

Mazvita was free of Joel. She had sought her dream first, ahead of him, and it was not possible that she would fail because of his particular instinct of dream. She allowed Joel to believe that she had no plans for the future. The deception was easy to accomplish, after all, in Harari the future was considered present and urgent. It suited Joel to believe that, to Mazvita, he was an unmistakable version of the future.

First she looked for work in all the wrong places, then she learnt that the most immediate work she could secure was not in the smoke-filled industrial areas, but in the affluent homes located on the other side of the hills, behind that yellow horizon she met every evening. Mazvita was definite that she had not come to the city simply to nurse the children of strangers. She would look for another kind of employment. She waited. She thought very hard of the employment she would have liked to secure. She dreamt of herself freed from Joel. She did not like to ask for money and felt uncomfortable when she had to. It was enough that she stayed in Joel's room, and ate the food he bought. Joel offered her respite while she searched hard for work. Mainly, she searched for who she was as she had realized that in the city, she was someone new and different, someone she had not met. Mazvita had to find her Harari. She had to find a voice with which to speak, without trying to hide from herself. She had to look up when someone spoke to her or else her newness betrayed her. She had to laugh with more abandon not with the restraint she had brought from Mubaira, and to walk too with firmer footsteps. Mazvita felt that freedom was here, but hidden to her. She had to find work first, then perhaps she might feel the release that she wished. She might even leave Joel, or if she stayed with him, it would be with the knowledge that she could leave when she desired it.

Mazvita hoped desperately to find a job in the city.

∞∞

17

Joel stirred her abandoned cry.

Mazvita was completely alone while she was with Joel. She closed her eyes and heard him move quickly above her. His movements were erratic as he sought her between the torn covers. A thin light sifted through the worn curtains and caught her arm over his head, in the darkness. She did not see the light. Her eyes were closed. Joel saw her eyes close and imagined the closing was about him, about his fingers touching her face, touching the curve of her eyes, searching her forehead. But Mazvita was alone. She imagined Joel was alone too. There were no words spoken between them.

Through the mist Mazvita smelt the stale grey blankets, the worn out mattress, the bell of a bicycle ring below the window, sewage water flowing across obstacles through a ditch beside the road, a man shouting angrily at a barking dog, a stone hitting one side of the wall.

Mazvita tried not to remember Joel as he rested above her. She tried to be alone but she could not be apart from him if she carried his face along, so she chose to forget Joel's face. It was hard to forget Joel. Mazvita buried Joel in the mist. The burying was difficult because Joel would not keep still. Mazvita turned her face from Joel as he moved towards her. She turned her face downward to the pillow, but he turned her face back towards himself. He released her neck from his grasp. She closed her eyes tighter and waited. She waited till she felt him pull her legs towards him, till he rested almost still, over her. He was motionless and heavy above her. If she moved slightly he would begin to move again. He gathered his strength from her calm. She remained quiet to accommodate him. If she moved just then, he would turn away, cursing and telling her to be still. She must be still when he desired pause. She welcomed this brief moment when he rested in an undisturbed quiet. Then she cried.

He felt her tremble beneath him and shift her legs a little, away from him. She heard herself cry. She cried till only she could be heard. Joel interrupted her crying with his breathing. She felt him breathe. He did not speak but held her tighter towards himself. She did not feel his actions at all, though he truly held her tight. She heard only her cry which expanded into the hollow spaces within her, into the silence she had conceived for herself, into the past of her memory. She lingered in her remembrance. The cry was a divine healing in which she stood alone, and whole. The cry was a triumph of her will, prolonged and full of her weeping, full of her laughter. She did not understand why she needed to laugh when the moment was so painful for her but she laughed in a breathless, broken spasm, in a distressful abandon. The laughter mixed with her tears. It was Joel she laughed at, she was sure. So when her laughing had struggled enough with her crying she reached her arms towards Joel and held him close to her breast till her tears fell downward past her temples and made the pillow wet. The mist fell from her eyes and she saw Joel's clothes that were pegged to the walls saw Joel, fallen asleep.

Mubaira was so far away it vanished from memory. Mazvita remembered the cry she had heard above Joel's anxious breath, heard above the paraffin that spread in the room, the soot, above the darkness growing in the room, the roof, above herself. Mazvita listened above the whirls of days and months that separated her from Mubaira. But Mazvita did not understand that the cry had defeated the silence in her body, that the cry was a release dangerous and regrettable. The cry was not the lulling freedom she sought. After her discovery Mazvita would once again long that the solitude had protected her, long that the hollow spaces within her had remained hollow, the silence supreme.

∞∞

18

The city women conjured freedom from chaos. They had red lips. Their carnival was new and persistent, for the women could be trusted to awaken the dead. The women proposed incredible assignations. They showed their capacity for absurdities, for building altars to wounded dreams. The vision they offered to the initiate was freeing and enticing. Prayers rose unsung from their lush lips. It was really not so hard to understand. The curious let the women pass in hordes, and stared at their threatening shoulders, and their surprised eyebrows. The brave followed them in equally evocative disguises, carrying even stranger pronouncements on their faces. It was not clear whether the women sought speech or silence, peace or war, with such masks. There was an elaborate secret, no doubt, for the gesture itself was astounding. They chose red for the colour of their fantastic realizations.

What uncommon deities were resurrected by the women! Red mud was spread beneath dreaming eyes. The carnival was barefaced and unbelievable, full of mimicry and death. The war was articulated in masks of dream and escape. It found expression in terror and courtship, in an excited sensuality, in figures speechless and dead. Guns soured the sky with black smoke.

The women picked their colours from a burning sun, from the lips of white women, then offered their bodies as a ransom for their land, their departed men, their corrupted rituals of birth. This bold and frantic gesture marked the ceremony for beginnings. In the silence that followed their transformation the women cried loud and clear and painted their nails a rhythmic red. The carnival was necessary and complete, so they lay in their dead bodies which they had rejected in the heightening clamour of the voices of their men, in the turmoil of fainthearted whispers.

The year was 1977.

∞∞

19

Joel. A stirring, of nausea, circling and turning. Mazvita lay still on the bed. It was dark in the room. She lay still and tried to bury the child inside her body. Mazvita buried the child. She would keep the child inside her body, not give birth to it. Joel must not discover that her body had betrayed them like this.

Joel. She could not think about Joel and the pregnancy together. Joel definitely would not want to hear about it. They had not agreed on any kind of permanency. If she was pregnant, then it was best to keep the knowledge to herself.

She had not thought the right thoughts to keep this child away. How could she have conceived the child without some knowledge in the matter? It burdened her, this surreptitious birth. Mazvita rejected the baby because it pulled her back from her design to be free. Harari was cramped and relentless. She did not imagine where she would give birth in this chaos of voices, of dancing voices. Her stomach heaved into her mouth. She leaned over the bed and vomited into a dish resting on the side of the bed. Her eyes burned with bitter tears. She held the nausea in her mouth, deep into her body. The burning spread down her throat. She hoped the burning would stop so that she could think, make precise decisions.

Mazvita buried the child. Joel would never know a thing about it.

Joel. The idea of giving Joel a child made her laugh, though she felt miserable. He had made no promises to her. Joel could leave whenever he wanted. She could leave when she wanted. So far she wanted to stay. A child interfered with her decision to stay.

Mazvita crouched beside the bed and vomited into the basin. The pain tightened around her chest, twisted, and rested there. If she moved her body forward, she was sure the pain would be unbearable, so she held her hands close to her chest, and remained still. She kept the vomiting inside her chest. The pain coiled and fastened above her stomach. She writhed, turned, and leaned once more into the basin. Her nostrils filled with mucus and she pressed her face on the bed and wiped her nose on the coarse grey blanket. She pressed her face hard on the bed, her body held down. Her face itched from the blanket and her eyes watered. She sneezed and curled upward from the bed. She knelt with her face still pressed on the bed. Mazvita brought her forehead to her knees. She was curled stiffly on the bed. She grew silent. Mazvita buried the child in her body.

She carried the basin outside. She rinsed the basin, slowly and carefully, under the tap outside the toilet, her legs stiff and weak. She walked slowly, painfully, back into the house. She sank on the bed and coughed terribly. Her arms ached. Her forehead grew wet. Her arms trembled, resting over her breasts. She shivered. Mazvita was cold and afraid.

Her thoughts wandered everywhere. She remembered Nyenyedzi, but quickly thought of Joel. It was better to think of Joel than of Nyenyedzi. She thought again of Nyenyedzi. The memory frightened her. She pulled Joel's shirt from a suitcase filled with unwashed clothes, under the bed, and thought of Joel. Joel. She remembered Nyenyedzi.

Mazvita thought of Joel. The child belonged to Joel. At least that was a beginning. She replaced Nyenyedzi with Joel. She replaced Joel with Nyenyedzi. She thought of Joel. She grew faint and lay still once more on the bed. It shocked her that she was expecting birth, that she would be a mother. She had not been concerned with birth. She had simply not thought about it. "Nyenyedzi," she called.

She had no doubt of her calamity.

Joel, again.

∞∞

20

She found herself on the bus, not yet resolved on her destination, but ready to go somewhere. The bus stood still. Mazvita waited anxiously at the back, cramped in the last seat on the bus. The seat was covered with the cages and the boxes and the pillows and the plant seeds. This indiscriminate pile towered behind her. She shared her seat with two women who fanned themselves with flat knitted baskets. They were older women. They swung their heavy arms in wide arcs and frowned at the heat. Mazvita kept the baby tied to her back. The women looked at Mazvita curiously. They looked at the baby whose head was covered with a white napkin. The napkin dropped from the mother's neck where it was firmly tied.

Mazvita maintained a detached pose. She did not greet the women. She held her face in an unwelcoming gaze. She raised her neck and kept it stiff and unreasonable. The pose was strenuous and surprising. She needed some kind of pose, she was sure. She needed new and untried gestures, and so she started with her neck, because that was where she felt most of her pain, that was where she felt she was living. The baby rested below her neck. She released the napkin and tied it up again, much more firmly. She could hardly breathe. It was not enough. She made another knot above the first. She could not afford to be discovered.

She pulled her neck up, above the heads of the two women. She opened her eyes wide and tried hard to keep them open. She had to keep her world in focus, or else it would change shape. She sorrowed in profuse echoes of dismay and loneliness. It was like that for her. Mostly, she feared her world would move into another room in which the door was tightly shut against her. She had conceived of such a deceptive manoeuvre while waiting outside the bus. Then, she feared that her world might enter the bus and leave her out of it. She had the wretched feeling of following her world around, with her eyes. It was hard for her to establish disguises that would permit her to be unrecognizable to her world, so that she could follow it successfully. It meant becoming a stranger to herself, first of all. Her eyes, therefore, were vital to her survival.

She could not afford to be unwary, to pause. There was such tension below her temples, such a confusion of racing footsteps. She had had to run when she thought she saw all traces of her world vanish. She hated the sound of her own footsteps because they grew upon each other, and she heard the footsteps when she ran this morning, and then she ran again, away from them, into another chaotic pattering. There was so little space inside her, nowhere for the sound of her feet to vanish. She stood still whenever she could. She grew stiff.

So, she held her neck up, or at least thought she did, though in truth, she sat curled in a miserable hump of fear, her shoulders crushed. Her head leaned towards the window and knocked on it repeatedly. Her head dipped down. Her head swung sideways. Her head hung towards her back, towards her child. Her right hand was held stiffly in front of her, the fingers curled sideways, as though she meant to throw something out through the window but the gesture had turned too heavy for her. She seemed waiting for assistance, but her fingers were empty, and so no one offered to help. Her fingers remained in that awkward frozen motion. Her eyes closed into mere slits through which she allowed the world to squeeze in, and she saw everything in a blur. Her faintness increased as the heat thickened in the bus, as her vision dissipated. She might have chosen that moment to die.

Then she heard an old man play the *mbira*.

The old man sat curled mid-way in the crowded bus, along the aisle. He was squeezed narrowly on the edge of the seat. He held the *mbira* possessively above his lap, and played. The *mbira* sat in one half of dried shell, a calabash. This shelter made the sound fall backwards, towards the back of the bus, where Mazvita waited. The gesture was unexpected and lavish. The sound reached her in generous waves of sustenance. Mazvita waited in a smooth and silent gaze. She turned her eyes from the window to the *mbira* and she cupped her fingers and held them forward. Her hands were still and seeking. The two women stared at her in amazement. Her eyebrows softened into arches of wonder. Her lips softened. The tightness disappeared along her neck. The skin on her neck grew smooth. The *mbira* was a revelation, a necessary respite. Mazvita waited with cupped hands.

The people in the bus continued their chatter, they laughed loud, told their children to sit still, coughed from the dust that fell in through the open windows ... Mazvita listened through that din of voices and received the *mbira* sound, guided it towards herself. She held her fingers tightly together. It fell in drops, the sound, into her cupped hands. She found the *mbira*. It was beneficent. The sound came to her in subduing waves, in a growing pitch, in laps of clear water. Water. She felt the water slow and effortless and elegant. She breathed calmly, in the water. The *mbira* vibrated through the crowd, reached her with an intact rhythm, a profound tonality, a promise graceful and simple. She had awakened.

It was a moment too exquisite to bear and she folded her arms across her breast and closed her eyes tightly, for the joy was reckless and free, stirring and timeless. A lapse, and the *mbira* hid from her. She searched frantic and forlorn through the growing voices, searched and listened. She remembered the first notes of the sound she had heard. She found the *mbira* held in her fingers. She caught the *mbira* but it was elusive when it chose, thinned into slow sudden drops like melting heavy clay and she waited in a gasp so finely protected, waited in a calm and steady embrace of shadow and sound. The moment was precious. It hung on a delicate spot below her neck, at the back of her neck. The sound looped in waves over her head, curled downward, sunk deep into her chest where she had been irrevocably wounded, touching her gently and faithfully, tenderly and with mercy. There was forgiveness because she longed for it. There was forgiveness as she desired it, reconciliation and dream. She heard the *mbira* grow loud, move nearer to her, nearer to her dream. She waited in waves of suspenseful wish and longing, in rays of supple joy. She sat still, waited though she knew deep down that her waiting was futile and misguided. The moment was intimate, irresistible and plentiful. She had longed so hard she had forgotten this was longing and yearning and desire. She remembered. The *mbira* was a splendid remembrance. She fought for a memory brilliant as a star, but there was darkness so deep and silent, and now, this glorious searching sound visited her, sought her out, found parts of her which were still whole, which held some sweetness and longing. The *mbira* grew loud and heavy like a thick shadow. It grew loud to bursting and she retreated. She could not risk such climactic yet hopeless tributes. She heard the sound encroach, poised and inviting. The *mbira* covered her across her shoulders, crept into the hidden spaces between her fingers.

She felt a movement. She allowed herself to hope. Mercy. Mercy. She waited for a moment merciful with release for the *mbira* held out a promise. She welcomed the *mbira* which brought to her a sky flaring with waves of white cloud. The *mbira* led her across a white sun. She waited for the sound to circle her with a new promise of freedom. Her arms trembled because she feared waiting. Her eyes opened bright and full of hope. She waited eagerly and trembling. Then the sound died. It died in slow undecided rhythms, as though someone hit hard at the instrument with a fist. The notes collapsed.

She looked up.

∞∞

21

When the sun began licking Mazvita's face she could smell the paraffin in the room. She had not slept. She always noticed the paraffin stove as soon as there was enough light in the room. She woke to the reeking smell. The stove rested on a raised platform at a corner of the room, where it was held tightly on a small wooden box.

Yesterday she had opened and pushed new cords into the stove, pushed them forward. Her fingers smelt of paraffin. She hated the lingering smell, the burnt smell of the smoke as it filled the room, entered into the food, tarnished everything. Clothes were hung in another corner of the room, along a line of pegs against the wall. The clothes, like the walls, bore the paraffin smell. They hung limp and dark with the paraffin. The house was small and ready to burst into flame. The blaze would begin from her fingers. They carried such a continuous stench. She imagined the flames lighting that limited room. The smell entered everything. Paraffin, life in Harari, life with Joel. She thought, she breathed, she slept. The paraffin was inescapable.

Running footsteps covered the tarred road, and Joel woke up. People were running to catch buses and travel the distance into the city. She could imagine them, shadows in the half-light carrying their food-tins that were filled with last night's left-overs; a bit of meat, some sadza, and perhaps a piece of bread added hurriedly by a concerned wife. She was not a wife, not in that specific sense. There were not many wives, like that, in Harari. Lighter footsteps, and the soft chatter of women going to their jobs in the city. She could never tell Joel. She buried the child. She was submerged in her secrets, and she breathed hard, like drowning. She had died silently with the thoughts she kept to herself. She could not hold her breath, like this, for much longer. Joel.

Joel snored oppressively beside her, she thought he had woken up. Had she not heard him stir? She could not bear to wake him for work. She could not stand the sound of him, or the smell of him. It surprised her that they lay so close to each other's dreams, and did not know each other's secrets. Did Joel not see that her stomach had grown, that she ate less, that her face had fallen. Did he know nothing of what she suffered? He groaned, and she turned away from him. He groaned and turned, rolling over to her side of the bed, as though to push her off.

Mazvita held her hands against his sweaty back, creating a barrier across which he could not move. Even this action that protected her from falling off the bed pained her, and as he settled again into restful sleep, she let him go. She hated to think of the baby. She thought of the baby. She passed a searching hand over her stomach. Her stomach stiffened. She swallowed the harsh paraffin smell.

She balanced carefully on the edge of the bed, suspended in the memory of their first encounter.

∞∞

22

Joel ignored the baby. It was not his. He wanted the baby to disappear.

Mazvita had deceived him. Her deception was final and inexcusable. He had no doubt that she knew about the baby, hid the fact from him, because she was desperate. He forgot all about the innocence he celebrated in her. She was like any other woman. He saw her pretending to fall off the bicycle when they first met. She had been so clever. The baby arrived seven months after they had met. Joel did not believe that Mazvita had not known anything about the baby.

Mazvita was as surprised as he was, and felt disgraced by the way her body had betrayed her. She wished the baby belonged to Joel. The baby belonged to her alone. She did not understand how the baby had chosen her like that, creeping into her life, surprising her. She had woken up one morning with a strong sense of something irretrievable and wrong. She felt a bitterness on her tongue, in her throat. She ignored the feeling for days, though she grew dizzy and weak and could not swallow food. Always, when she got out of bed, her knees shook and failed to support her weight.

She told Joel about the baby and her misery.

In all the months she waited she closed the thought of the baby away.

She simply waited. The waiting was separate from the baby. She waited only for the bitterness to leave her tongue. She hated that bitterness which made her tongue heavy, which made her unable to sleep. If Joel did not want the baby, she would also not think about it.

She wanted to stay with Joel. She had settled into the easy undemanding method of their life together. She had been looking for employment and felt an eagerness concerning what awaited her in the future. She was sure to find a place to work. She had meant to surprise Joel, to surprise herself with her success. Her freedom came in soothing waves of forgetting, in her increasing distance from Mubaira. She entered slowly into her life in the city, but with unmistaken resolutions.

Then the baby arrived, just like that. She had no name for the baby. A name could not be given to a child just like that. A name is for calling a child into the world, for acceptance, for grace. A name binds a mother to her child. A name is for waiting, for release, an embrace precious and permanent, a promise to growing life. She had no promises to offer this child. Mazvita could not even name the child from the emptiness which surrounded her. She simply held the child, and fed her from her breast. The child grew in a silence with no name. Mazvita could not name the silence.

It was futile, remaining with Joel like this. Mazvita understood that she had to leave. She stayed on. He became violent with his words. He chose his words well, for he wanted her to leave. She stayed. She needed more than words to initiate her departure. She knew she had to leave, would leave.

Then one morning, she woke up in a sweat.

∞∞∞

23

1977. People were known to die amazing deaths. Natural deaths were rare, unless one simply died in sleep.

The people on the bus knew the truth about their own dying, but they had a capacity to evade uncomfortable realities. It was a risk to be on a journey, to travel. Travelling was a suspension of all pretence to freedom. Travelling made living real. The road was cluttered with dead bodies and held no promise of growth. A road was not for pursuing destinations: a road was another manifestation of death.

1977. It was a time for miracles. If you arrived at your destination still living, then you prayed desperately to continue to live. It was hard in those rural landscapes. There were all kinds of horizons witnessed, all kinds of sunsets. The sky was embroidered with new suns, for it burnt even in the middle of the night. The sunsets were brilliant and unimaginable. A war has amazing sunsets.

1977. Everyone was an accomplice to war.

The war made them strangers to words. They shaped any truth which comforted them. The war changed everything, even the idea of their own humanity. They were shocked at what they witnessed and lived through, what they were capable of enduring, the sights they witnessed. They welcomed silence. If they spoke with energy and abandon, it was to fill the empty spaces left by those who had died marvellous deaths, who had vanished in the midst of their journeying. The war made the people willing accomplices to distortions – distortions solitary and consoling.

People lived with their feet off the ground, though they indeed travelled. There are stranger truths in the world. The war made the people generous with their bodies. They offered their bodies for their improbable journeying. They were welcomed, and feasts prepared for them, even before they entered the road. It was known they were coming, and those who knew about their coming welcomed them, days before they arrived. It was not known what would happen to the body as it journeyed. A journey was not to be trusted. Only the promise to arrive could be resurrected and protected.

The travellers were not surprised when the bus sank downward, as though a new weight had been added to the roof. The bus stopped in the middle of the road. The stopping was abrupt, threw them forward, and they fell back into their seats.

They searched the opaque windows, and saw through the dust the lines of police vehicle. The faces were brown and buried, indistinct, minute. The heads were missing from the shoulders, the arms chopped off. The windows were thick with dust. The people searched fearfully behind the sheltering glass in a temporary refuge for their fear.

A policeman went round to the driver and spoke to him. The driver moved from his seat and descended the stairs to the door. He pushed hard at the door with his shoulder. The door flew open. Metal banged on metal. The driver leapt out of the bus, so did the conductor. The people sank further into their seats.

Mazvita. She watched a soldier standing under the dusty window. He held a gun close to his body, close to his face. His face was scarred. She stared at the scars on the face of the soldier. She wanted to stay on the bus when she saw everyone move down the passage, lifting their heavy boxes and their wares. The face she thought she had recognized moved towards her and knocked hard with the gun against the window, so she moved forward, like everyone else. She had hoped the soldier would know her.

"Bring all your bags," a voice bellowed into the bus.

The conductor leapt to the roof of the bus and untied the goods. The untying was laborious because the goods had been tied in firm knots for the long journey, to resist the uneven road. A soldier barked at the conductor. He worked at the ropes, in that heat, in that fear, in that promiseless sky. He searched his pocket rapidly, found a knife and sliced through the knots. The suddenness of release sent some of the goods falling on one side of the bus, and the driver ran forward. A table tumbled and crushed on the side of the road, sideways, its legs curved inward.

The soldiers rummaged furiously through the goods, tossed garments in every direction, whispered endless prophecies, asked the women to stand on one side of the road, with the children. Mazvita. Her eyes were clear of tears.

∞∞

24

Mazvita dreamt the child had vanished. She screamed till Joel woke her. He insisted, even in the middle of the night, in the midst of her violent dream, that she must leave on that morning.

"Leave me," he said. He swung his body away from her. She heard his knees hit against the wall. He pulled his legs back, and slept. He slept while she turned and tossed.

She offered to take the baby away to her home, and then come back to him. "That is good," he said. He was so quick with his answer she knew there was no hope of finding him waiting. Instead, she conceived a deep hatred for this man who found it impossible to accept her and the child. He denied her an opportunity she had sought, to grow. She did not ask for love from him, just acceptance. Instead, Joel interrupted her every thought. He had wearied of her presence.

It was as though she was living with two men. When she thought of Nyenyedzi, she loved the child deeply. She called the child Nyenyedzi, in her dream, because the child was a boy. When she thought of Joel, she wanted the child to go away. She had no memory of being close to this child, even while it grew inside of her. She had no memory of this child growing inside her. She fed the child from her breast, and turned her eyes away. Her breasts felt heavy with the milk for this child. The child had brought its own milk. It had definite plans about its own survival. Joel stayed from her milk and her child. Mazvita grew thin with her thought. She had such dreams.

She dreamt of Nyenyedzi. She dreamt of his tenderness and promises. She wished that she had stayed with him as he had asked. She wished she had known about the child before she left. She would not have left. She longed for Nyenyedzi. She dreamt that she met him and showed him the child. He rejected the child saying it was not his. He would not accept her. It did not matter to him how much she had suffered to bring his child into the world. Nyenyedzi stayed away from her milk. Mazvita had no memory of giving birth to this child. Joel told her it was her child. Mazvita held the baby close to her breast.

One morning, after she had again woken dripping in a sweat, Mazvita sat by the window and watched the child as it lay on the bed, in that room small and dark. The walls were dark, the curtains hung in shreds of dim light. She heard the soft whir of the paraffin stove, because she had lit it to boil some water. She heard the flame blow against the surface of the kettle. The room, the curtains, the bed. She held her nose in distaste. Mazvita disliked the paraffin smoke which she had to rub off the pots.

The lower part of her right palm was black with oily smoke.

∞∞

25

The City.

Clothes hung on wooden figures, on women still, thin and unmoving. The figures offered no names, no memory. The past had vanished. Perhaps they offered beginnings, from the outside in. One could begin with a flattering garment, work inwards to the soul. It was better to begin in sections, not with everything completed and whole. It led to such disasters, such unreasoned ambition. So the dresses hung limp on the women, offering tangible illusions, clothed realities. These glassed and protected women had long brown hair and red lips and arms stretched, offering a purchasable kind of salvation. The figures had a rare insight into bodies, with no breasts, yet their children stood with them in equal poses of divinity. The children held plastic arms towards their mothers. The children wore lace. They wore bright red ribbons. It was difficult to understand the exchange the children offered because it was so clear that they had not begun to live, that their parents, standing holier above them, had at least some form of pretence – long smooth necks held out to the day, heads bent slightly inward, as though they served tea. It was like that with the figures, an austere reality, fixed, with handbags held across arms stiff and long. Silent eyes fixed on passers-by. The eyes saw and spoke nothing. The eyes were voiceless. They burrowed, ate their own bodies.

The ritual was cruelly imitated.

26

"When are you leaving?" his tone was abrupt. She dared not answer him. Instead, she fed the baby. He looked quickly round the room. His eyes darted over the head of the baby, darted across her breasts, across the window into the dark. He skirted, swung onto the bed, and pulled a magazine. He flipped through pages.

Mazvita fed the baby slowly and patiently. She observed Joel's every quick move. She saw a finger pass over his tongue, then pages flip, read backward. He snapped his fingers, accompanying some tune held in his head, placed the book under his shoulder where he rested on the bed, closed his eyes, snapped his fingers in a fast rhythm she could not follow. He closed her out. Whistled. He snapped and whistled.

Joel jumped up from the bed and opened the window. The window creaked. The window creaked, and closed. The pages rustled.

Mazvita fed the baby slowly and patiently.

The bed creaked. The question leapt at her. Mazvita turned her face slowly towards him. She sat on a mat on the floor. He looked, looked away, looked again. Feet swung from the bed to the ground. Her heart beat fast because she thought he had made an irrevocable decision that excluded her immediately. She moved the baby from her breast.

"When are you leaving?"

Joel moved back to the small window and lifted the curtain. A dog howled in the distance. Joel let the curtain fall. He stood with his back resting against the wall. He took several quick steps around her, cast a brisk but penetrating stare at the baby. He vanished behind her.

She gasped. His voice was swift.

"Leave. Tomorrow," he said with a prompt emphasis.

Her decision came to her slowly. When it did come, she was not sure that the decision had been entirely her own.

∞∞

27

She had stopped thinking of Nyenyedzi and Joel. She thought of Joel. She remembered the morning, running. She no longer thought of that man while she was awake. She kept trying to find his face and all she felt were his arms over her legs, pulling her down. She was sure that if she remembered his face, she could free herself of remembering him. She could replace his face with another, with beginnings. She searched for his face. She felt arms circling her legs, coiling over her, and she fell onto the stranger. She fell on his outstretched legs. It was as though she had tripped and fallen down, except she had felt the pull on her legs. He pulled at her. She did not cry but struggled slowly against him. He whispered in harsh lulling tones, whispered persuasively, demandingly, and pulled her roughly towards him. He whispered that he did not have time to talk to her. He whispered about the things he did not have time to do. "Maybe you have time for all these things," he informed her. He spoke with his face turned from her. She thought only of being buried, of dying slowly after he had killed her. She believed she had died except she felt his hands moving over her shoulders. He was determined to discover parts of her that were hidden to herself.

The morning covered her eyes, her feet. He parted her feet and rested above her. His face was turned away from her. He kept his face hidden, and whispered repeatedly to her. He tore at her dress, pulled her legs away from her. He removed her legs from her body, and she lay still, not recognizing her legs as her own. The mist hung on her forehead, behind the armed man, only his hands rested on her shoulders and kept her pinned on the ground. He slid above her, beneath the shelter of the mist.

Then she ran. She heard him behind her when she started to run into the morning. She ran but the morning was full of his whispers, of his arms moving beneath her body, of his hidden face, of his fingers pulling at her feet, of his stale and damp clothing. She ran from him, ran from the things he had whispered between her legs.

She ran from the rising mist, from the morning.

She forgot about Nyenyedzi and Joel. She remembered the mist and the whispers.

∞∞

28

This hole is so deep and so old and heavy on my back. Joel, this body is not me sinking into this hole so deep and dark. Where can I go and remain whole? Who will help me carry this pain? Where will I speak this tale, with which mouth for I have no mouth left, no fingers left, no tears to drink. Let me thirst and die. Let me lie down and die because I have died in this sleep. What is it that came to visit that left footmarks here and there and everywhere? It left its skin right there on my path for me to nest under. I will be buried in a skin unknown and strange. Joel, I hear a fly buzzing all around. It is buzzing around the head of my child. Is that the hole dug for me, so deep, and that fly buzzing over my head sent from that hole? Who will hear my song? Who will carry it for me this pain and this suffering heavy on my back? I have turned and turned in my sleep dreamt of mountains such mountains growing on my back? Let me walk onto that mountain growing on my back...

She had not anticipated such a hollow feeling, such emptiness. The child brought to hear such powerlessness she could hardly move forward. Mazvita could not remain where she was because Joel forbade it. He suggested that she move backward, into the past, Her instinct was to dream new dreams. There was such a heaviness in her arms. Mazvita longed to release the heaviness that made her unable to spread her arms and embrace the future. She wanted her arms but they were heavy with the child. Mazvita sought the path that led her here. She gathered her footprints till they disappeared from her vision. The past was more inventive than she was, laid more claim on what belonged to it. The baby had chosen her, risen above its own frailty in order to hinder her.

Mazvita felt betrayed.

∞∞

29

The bus plunged into clouds of thickening red dust. Mazvita was surprised to hear laughter on the bus. It was as though the laughing had moved from inside her into the bus, into the mouths of strangers. She had preferred the laughter when it was silent, and completely hers. Now she had to laugh together with the strangers. She heard the two women in the seat ahead.

Mazvita had to laugh with the women too. It was not clear why they laughed, but one of the women pointed to a cloud of heavy dust coming through the window and leaned forward to fight against it. But the window had tightened and the woman had to fight hard to close the window. When she finally pulled back her face was covered with the dust. Her face was red. The people laughed. The people in the bus laughed about the dust covering the woman. Their laughter must be different from hers, then. Mazvita did not share the safety and certainty held in their laughter so she felt assured that they had not stolen her secret. Mazvita felt rescued. She searched through the dust covering the window, through the clouds growing outside as the bus journeyed forward. She would arrive soon.

She turned her eyes back to the bus and found the women still laughing. Mazvita knew enough about her own survival to know that she had to laugh with the others, to throw her arms and meet those of the other women half way across the seat, to glance at the men and see how they laughed at the woman. To laugh with the men. It was a chance to dispel suspicions regarding her apparent silence. It was difficult for her. She leaned forward and protected a pain beneath her chest. She could not laugh with the women, loud like that, when the pain threatened repeatedly. She closed her eyes.

Mazvita closed her eyes and saw the dust all over the woman's face. The woman had returned from the window to her seat. The woman followed Mazvita into her dream, into the place she chose to hide. Mazvita could not keep the woman from following her. She remembered the soldier she had seen through the window. The soldier must have shot this woman because he had stood on just this side of the road. No. The woman was still living. It was only that she, Mazvita, had closed her eyes to keep the woman away. There had been no soldier on the side of the road yet Mazvita remembered that the soldier had held a gun. Where had she met the soldier, then? Mazvita felt a dizzying and painful motion stir inside her, with her memory. She folded her chest and felt the baby shift on her back. It was important to keep the strange woman away from her. The woman remained far away, beyond Mazvita's closed eyes. She must not think of the woman. The woman had been killed by the soldier. The soldier had killed her, after... Mazvita could not remember the event after which the woman had met her death. Certainly, death had come slowly to the woman. Mazvita told herself to remain calm, though her heart beat rapidly. It would not be long before she, Mazvita, left this bus. She was safe. She must keep the dead woman away from her thoughts. Dust fell over the woman's hair which turned red like the clouds outside.

Mazvita had not spoken throughout the trip. Now she moved her lips slowly and painfully, though no one listened to her, not even the woman who followed her into her thought. Mazvita spoke about waiting for the bus. The waiting had not been for long. Mazvita spoke about the tie she had left on the bed. Joel must not miss his tie. She could not remember if she had left the tie on the bed or on the table. She could not remember clearly and felt her heart beat beneath her chest. Perhaps she had brought the tie with her. Where was the tie if she had brought it with her? She should have talked to the woman who sold her the white apron. She was sure the woman would have listened. She saw the woman smile and hand her the folded apron. The woman folded the apron slowly and carefully, as though she acknowledged the long distance Mazvita had to travel before unfolding it again. Mazvita received the apron and held it in one hand. She pulled the hand over her chest. She did not wait long to unfold the apron. She saw her child within every fold of that apron, as it fell open towards the ground. Mazvita moved her lips slowly as she remembered the apron unfolding. She heard the women laugh in the background and thought it was only her own voice murmur into her memory, murmur softly and mutely.

Then Mazvita saw again the strange woman carrying the dust on her face. Mazvita did not understand how the woman had continued to follow her through the things she said to herself, that she expressed in her quiet gestures. Yet she had felt the woman constantly there, seeking to find her. The woman sought to discover the things Mazvita left unsaid. Mazvita saw the woman lean towards her and tell her to remove the child from her back. Mazvita heard the awful cry leave her, heard the bus turn to silence. Mazvita had not wanted to awaken like that. Again she cried pitifully. The woman told her to release the child from her back and allow the child to play. Why did she not allow the child to play. She was a cruel woman to her child, keeping her on her back all the way on the bus. A child must not be kept on the back for such a long time, and in this heat. Did she not know that this heat could kill her child. She must remove that napkin from the baby's head, at least. Mazvita spoke, the woman spoke. Their voices were one. The woman spoke with Mazvita's voice. Mazvita had not heard her voice for a long time and it shocked her to hear her own voice come to her from the woman, so clearly pronounced. Mazvita laughed. She laughed with the voice of the woman, which was also her own voice. Mazvita cried to the woman to keep quiet but the woman leaned over the seat and repeated the same words, in the same voice that belonged to Mazvita.

As the woman spoke, as Mazvita spoke, Mazvita felt an awful piercing beneath her breasts. Her lips shivered with the cry that spread outward from her chest. It spread beneath her eyelids. Mazvita knew that the woman had stolen her thought and that there was no use fighting her. Mazvita answered that she would release the baby very soon. Mazvita answered with two voices, both of which were hers. Then she felt the woman bend forward and start to untie her apron. She was a daring woman indeed. She had such fire in her eyes, such a determined frown. Mazvita allowed the woman to untie the apron. She could not stand against such a determination. After all, the determination was her own. She wondered why she would do a foolish thing as allowing a strange woman to expose her, to uncover her secrets, to speak with her own voice, but she felt tired of fighting. She longed for a comforting anonymous face. She longed to be discovered, to be punished, to be thrown out of the bus. It was better for her than to continue on this journey. The dust spread evenly over the window, in thick red clouds. She could not survive the journey. Mazvita felt the woman touch her beneath the chest. The arms belonged to Mazvita. Mazvita moved her own arms towards her chest. She rested the fingers over the knots and allowed the woman to proceed. She would not help the woman to uncover her. Mazvita's body rose up, against the woman. Mazvita had tied the apron tightly beneath her stomach. Again, she felt a tremor over her arms, and she cried weakly. The untying was difficult for the woman and she cursed as she struggled with the thick cloth. Mazvita was determined not to help the woman and held her fingers tightly over the knots. Mazvita closed her eyes again and felt the stranger free the child. The child fell from her back onto the seat and this woman with dust on her face this woman she thought was herself told her to hold onto the child. Mazvita took the child and held the child in her arms. The child's head had grown soft. The neck had grown wide. The child had been growing on her back. She did not recognize the face of her child. Mazvita tried to hide the neck of her child. She told the strange woman that her child was sick. She must keep her child on her back where it was quiet and safe. The woman seized the child from her and brought it to her own breast. She would feed the child because it was hungry. Why had she not fed the child in all their travelling. What kind of child slept so soundly when there was such a noise on the bus. Then the cry exploded in her again and Mazvita opened her eyes and found her fingers clasping the tied ends of the apron. The apron was still tied to her back. The knot held firmly above her breast. Mazvita reached cautiously and felt the baby still fastened on her back.

Mazvita turned to see that the woman was wiping her face with her scarf, and the wiping made the men laugh even more because it left the woman's head bare, and her hair was grey. The men laughed at the woman because her hair was grey. The women laughed with the men. Mazvita laughed with the women and the men. Her laughter was secret and whole.

Mazvita rubbed the dust, slowly, from her own eyebrows.

∞∞

30

Mazvita sat on the edge of the narrow bed, and held her hands tightly together. The baby lay in the middle of the bed.

Mazvita took the baby and rested a cold palm over its eyes.

She wanted the baby to close its eyes. Mazvita wept silently, because she knew that her desire for the baby to sleep was ill-conceived and harmful. Her heart beat so hard at her effort to suppress that inclination, but the desire lunged forward like something sweet and secret. She thought of sleep. She thought of loneliness and sleep. The feeling was overwhelming. She trembled beneath that thought. She closed her eyes and felt a cloud rest over her shoulders. Her shoulders felt heavy. She opened her eyes and thought of the child. She wanted to forget the child and creep back into that billow above her shoulders, crawl into a lethargic sleep.

She looked at the baby resting with its eyes opened. If the baby had fallen asleep right then she would have recovered from the madness that made her press her palm down, again, over the baby's eyes. Mazvita was still aware of her danger. The baby should have slept of its own accord right then, but it did not. She pressed her right palm softly, once more, over the baby. She felt the child's warm eyes under her palm.

That pressing granted her an elaborate and fierce energy to free herself from this baby, it drove her into a violent but calculated trance as she moved forward towards the child and picked it from the bed, picked it slowly and finally, picked it in sobs that rendered her body into half, in sobs. She picked the baby slowly, as though not to waken it. Her desire was to close the baby's eyes finally and truthfully. Mazvita sought her freedom in slender and fragile movements, finely executed.

Mazvita sung slow and dear to the baby that she felt was hers, was not hers, was hers, was not hers. She paused as though to comfort the child, touched it with one smooth gaze, as though to protect it. The child had deep bottomless eyes. She longed to close the eyes of her child, slowly and gently. The thought brought her an easy satisfaction, an exultant realization of a pleasure ephemeral but true. Joy beckoned in lilting waves of mercy and comfort.

Mazvita took a soft thin cloth and wrapped it over the child's eyes. The cloth smelt of milk. She had used the cloth to wipe the curdled milk from the side of the baby's mouth. The cloth fitted across the child's head, and she was able to tie it at the back. She made the knot very softly, whispering to the child to keep still. She made a soft painless knot that kept the child free from harm. The child listened to her slow cautioning movements, and kept still. This was a beginning. When she had completed this task she felt more sure of the direction in which she would proceed, she felt herself gifted and supreme, autonomous in all her decision, in her every gesture and action, and she breathed hard and inward and felt the air flow into her chest. She had closed the eyes of her child. Her breath returned to her in short repeated spurts.

She leaned forward and held the child's face in a lengthy and purposeful scrutiny. Mazvita moved forward once more, towards the child. Water broke from her forehead and fell over the child's eyes, which were hidden. It fell in dots over the milk cloth. The cloth was damp with the water from her forehead. Mazvita noticed the dampness and felt an intense loneliness meet her in that silent room. She got up in slow measured steps from the bed, leaving the child.

She returned to the bed and sat down. Her arms reached towards the child.

She was alone. She felt threatened somehow but did not understand all the permutations of her misery. Only that her arms waited, and that the dampness across the child's eyes had come from her. The baby belonged to her, and she was alone. She whispered softly, about her loneliness.

Her arms waited for the child.

She sat with the baby held in a blind-fold across her arms. Mazvita searched the room with her eyes. She did not quite remember being in this room before, though it was familiar. She searched, aware that the moment was vital and she could not let it pass without something gained towards her release, not when the moment had come to her like this, like sleep. The baby relaxed in Mazvita's tight grip, perhaps it had finally closed its eyes. But Mazvita missed the baby's signs of co-operation because she had already wandered far and distant. She had discovered and reached a completely new horizon.

Her determination was amazing. She stood outside her desire, outside herself. She stood with her head turned away from this ceremony of her freedom, from this ritual of separation. She saw nothing of the wildness in her actions, of the eyes dilating, of her furrowed brow, of her constricted face, of her elongated arms, of her shoulders stiff. She mistook her resolve for kindness. She saw nothing of her tears, yet she cried desperately in that triumph of her imagination, in that rejection of the things that were hers, that were of her body. Her forehead broke into ripples. Water fell from her forehead to her eyes, and blinded her.

Her rejection was sudden and fierce and total. She stood with the baby balanced on one arm. She took a black tie from a rack in a corner of the room and dropped it over the child's neck. It rested over the child in a huge loop, which, on another occasion, would have made her laugh. She did not pause. She claimed her dream and her freedom. She was winged and passionate. She drew the bottom end of the tie across the baby's neck. She pulled at the cloth while the baby remained blinded and trusting. She strained hard and confidently though this pulling choked her and blinded her and broke her back. It was bold, this pulling of the cloth and she held on till there was no cloth to pull because the cloth had formed one tight circle the smallest circle there was, and so there was no longer any use to her boldness. No use to her boldness because her boldness had brought a terrible silence into the room. There was absolutely no movement, no movement even from her own arms. She noticed first the stillness in her arms. She noticed her arms.

Bewildered and standing outside her own self she remembered some of her action towards this child. She had managed a constricting knot from which the child could not survive. She felt the neck break and fall over her wrist. She felt the bone at the bottom of that neck tell her that the child had died. The bone broke softly. The sound of it lingered long after she had heard it. The neck was broken. Still, she held the knot firmly between her fingers, for a while longer. She released the knot. The head swung back and fell onto her palm, because she had broken it. She had broken the neck of her child.

The head fell forward and she saw the top of the child's head. She saw the soft part of her child where she had been waiting for the hair to grow. She passed a cold hand over that soft dying part, and felt the softness still there. It had sunk inward, that soft part. It was bare and unprotected. The hair had not grown on it. It was bare that soft part of her child where the hair had not yet grown. Soft, and dying. She held the softness gently on her palm. The neck was broken. Her look as she held the face of the child was lulling and tranquil. She longed, tenderly, for the child's hair that she had not seen.

She kept the cloth over the child's eyes and placed the child back on the bed, where she had begun. She sought to discover the path she had taken towards this particular horror, but the memory hid from her. It came in flashes of a fathomless and heavy guilt. Her fingers felt cold and separate from her. She sat in painful isolation, convinced that what had happened was not true at all, yet, what was that blindfold on the child, when had she put it there? The unusual detail confirmed the horror in her head. A mountain grew in her head.

She was responsible for some horrible and irreversible truth concerning her actions. She held her breath tight, within her chest. There was a burning on her tongue. Her tongue seemed to grow in her mouth, into something large and unrecognizable. She could no longer breathe cleanly and regularly. The bitterness spread to her face, into her eyes. She closed her eyes and tried hard to collect her thoughts, concerning the child. She did not want to think of the child. She thought of the child.

She sat still, and wondered. She stood up. Her feet felt heavy but she took a step forward, dragged herself back towards the child. Her elbows ached tremendously. She fell forward, near where the baby lay. She slumped onto the bed, reared her neck forward and raised her arms. The action was unbearable. She untied the cloth from the child's eyes. The eyes were closed peacefully in sleep. She felt almost joyous because she recalled a moment when this was the simple fact she sought. She recalled such a moment. The child had closed its eyes willingly. The closing of the eyes was good, but she saw the neck collapse downward on the baby's chest. The neck was broken.

Perhaps the child was not dead. She carried the baby on her back. The child liked to be carried on the back. The child remained silent while Mazvita moved in quiet footsteps across the room. Mazvita moved back and forth, near the bed. She sung softly, her lips pursed slightly. She sung in mute tones, in muffled and confused cries, pleading, hoping the child would stir.

She felt the small head slide down towards her left shoulder and the move was silent and familiar. The child had fallen asleep. She had to hold the child up because it had fallen asleep in that awkward position, so she bent her back and leaned forward and re-arranged the baby and supported it with her cloth. She held the child's head up along her back with the cloth and went around the room because she wanted the child to sleep.

She sang a faint lullaby to which there were no words. She sang of dying mushrooms, the ones she had found.

Then she bent again and released the cloth. The baby slumped downward, curled into her back. She felt the child's silent fingers beneath her arms.

She had accomplished a tremulous vision. She was capable of brave pronouncements, still. She would bury her child in Mubaira, then she would die. She would go to Nyenyedzi and give him his child. It was his child. She left the tie on the bed, for Joel. The tie belonged to Joel. He must not miss it. She found the bus-station where she had arrived only a few months ago.

It fell in lumps, the milk. It fell from the baby's mouth.

∞∞

31

The bus continued to move.

Every sound seemed to listen for her, though she was the one who listened in a rare painful listening that crept across her back, kept still so painfully still the stillness made her sob a heavy sob that broke over her shoulders, trembled down to her feet, and she felt her toes turn cold, turn cold and still. She entered a bottomless ache that left her perspiring and gasping for one slice of moon, to heal her not regretfully, but with a brimming ululating sympathy. Bottomless, that ache, cold and still.

It was the stillness on her back, cloying and persistent, which bothered her, choked her, sent a small painful echo tearing across her breast, turned her lips a bursting black clay, clinging and cold. She felt her eyes sink into the darkness gathered somewhere beneath her forehead, beneath the eyebrows, a still cold darkness in which she was sure there was no recovery.

Her back was moist and heavy. The stillness called to her, soft, cold. She felt her toes tighten and grow stiff, felt her nails break and break tearing over her skin, felt her ankles burn an intense deep burning, licked with a flame she could not fathom, and she looked straight ahead, tried to hide from the sounds that surrounded her with a gay indifference, telling stories, free, unlike her who carried such a weight on her back.

She listened to every sound in her thought, and wept deep and slow for the stillness on her back, a heavy cold stillness that hugged her, spread its arms around her, with small cold fingers, so cold and small. It rested over her spine, this coldness. It tried to deceive her, for her back broke into sparkles of flame. A red spot of flame grew on her back, like life. She knew beyond that searing wave, she knew the beyond of it, the cold that was heavier than the heat, for the heat was light. It was light not like petals or sunshine or reveries. It was light like burning skin. It was heavy.

The bus was crowded. She heard everything in that crowded bus, but something larger than her listened to her, heard her, scorned her suffering. The something was mocking and spirited, she dared not find it out, it was something haunting and triumphant, enormous and penetrating. It was not possible that she had just suffered like that, without an audience. She deserved at least one ear into her secret.

Mazvita thought she heard a soft humble breath caress her back, a shifting spreading wetness like tears, warm and asking, then she panicked knowing that this was not life, but death.

∞∞

32

It is yesterday.

The trees are heavy with pod. There are no leaves on the trees, only twisting long pods. The leaves have fallen down. Trees sound with the wind beating against the branches, knocking the pods together. A dry sound, then stillness rattling, loud, between the hanging pods and the empty branches. Mazvita looks up. The pods are long and oval in the bare branches, large and full of clustered seed. Leaves fall in the arid air, race into the grasses in a promise of growth. She looks up and sees a purple flower tucked beneath the dry hanging branches, nestling into another season of flowering. The flower rests in a bare tortured tree, surviving, resisting the wind and shaking pods. Trees flatten and spread against the sky, their skin falling and folding to the ground. The trees grow across the sky. Mazvita walks through a narrow foot path held between the hills. Before, she must have looked up like this, just like this, learning to forget, bare and troubled.

If she had no fears, she could begin here, without a name. It is cumbersome to have a name. It is an anchor. It brings figures to her memory. It recalls this place to her, which, earlier, she has chosen to forget. Names inspire an entire childhood, faces reaching and touching. She wishes to forget the names that call her own name, then the hills would name her afresh. She would have liked to begin without a name, soundlessly and without pain. She is frightened. She has begun poorly, with too many visitations. She sees her mother, old, coming towards her, calling, "Mazvita!"

Mazvita looks up and sees the rocks small and many from deep in the valley deep grey, with stones spread between mounds of earth and bare trees. The stones are spread in the sky for the sky swallows everything, pulls one up, pulls the eyes. The hills are high and the sky grows from the mountains. The mountains push at her, push her from the path, against the burnt grass. New grass grows over the burnt grass. The rocks tumble down the mountain. It is not peaceful, but the sky makes the rocks seem harmless – mist grows over the hills and covers the rocks. Mazvita finds the path again. The mist fills her eyes and hides the sky. The mist is the sky. The mist is blue like the sky but she knows it is not the sky it is the mist. The mist is the sky and the rocks on the side of the hill. The sky tumbles and falls. The mist spreads and folds over the mountains, in layers, over the falling rocks. She walks in a blend of mist and rock, the sky falling over her shoulders, brimming from the mountains, over her head.

It is yesterday. Mazvita sees the smoke and hills. The huts are tucked in the hills, built among the rocks, with winding paths and thorny furrows between them. The huts are buried in the smoke. Mazvita moves slowly towards the huts, towards the smoke. The smoke tarnishes the horizon.

It is yesterday.

The village has disappeared. Mazvita can smell the burnt grass, though most of it has been washed away by the rain. The soil is black with the burnt grass. Mazvita gathers the burning grass. She will carry the burning grass with her. She will carry the voices that she remembers from this place, from the burning grass. She has not forgotten the voices. The broken huts are dark with the smoke and the mist falls gently over the empty walls.

Mazvita moves towards the huts. The smoke is long departed, but Mazvita can see it over the huts which have been burnt. It is yesterday. Mazvita walks in gentle footsteps that lead her to the place of her beginning. Mazvita bends forward and releases the baby from her back, into her arms.

The silence is deep, hollow and lonely.

∞∞